MY BODY IS PAPER

MY BODY IS PAPER

STORIES AND POEMS

GIL CUADROS

Foreword by Justin Torres
Afterword by Pablo Alvarez

EDITED BY
Pablo Alvarez
Kevin J. Martin
Rafael Pérez-Torres
Terry Wolverton

CITY LIGHTS BOOKS / SAN FRANCISCO

The following works have previously appeared in print:

An earlier version of "Hands" was published in the exhibition catalog *transcend AIDS: work by Los Angeles artists with HIV/AIDS*, December 1-17, 1995.

Earlier versions of "Coming Out" and "Last Supper" were published in *Queer in Aztlan: Chicano Male Recollections of Consciousness and Coming Out.*

"If She Could" and "Parrots" were published in *Gulf Coast Journal* 36.1.

An earlier version of "Birth" was published in *His 2: Brilliant New Fiction by Gay Writers* and in *Queer in Aztlán: Chicano Male Recollections of Consciousness and Coming Out.*

Cover photo of Gil Cuadros by Laura Aguilar, © The Trust of Laura Aguilar of 2016
Cover design by Jeff Clark
Text design by Patrick Barber

Library of Congress Cataloging-in-Publication Data

Names: Cuadros, Gil, author. | Torres, Justin, 1980- writer of foreword. | Alvarez,
    Pablo (Assistant professor in women and gender studies), writer of afterword,
    editor. | Martin, Kevin (Kevin J.), editor. | Pérez-Torres, Rafael, editor. |
    Wolverton, Terry, editor.
Title: My body is paper : stories and poems / Gil Cuadros ; foreword by Justin
    Torres ; afterword by Pablo Alvarez ; edited by Pablo Alvarez, Kevin Martin,
    Rafael Pérez-Torres, Terry Wolverton.
Description: San Francisco : City Lights Books, 2024.
Identifiers: LCCN 2023058662 (print) | LCCN 2023058663 (ebook) |
    ISBN 9780872869097 (paperback) | ISBN 9780872869103 (epub)
Subjects: LCGFT: Short stories. | Poetry.
Classification: LCC PS3553.U22 M9 2024 (print) | LCC PS3553.U22 (ebook) |
    DDC 813/.54—dc23/eng/20240202
LC record available at https://lccn.loc.gov/2023058662
LC ebook record available at https://lccn.loc.gov/2023058663

City Lights Books are published at the City Lights Bookstore
261 Columbus Avenue, San Francisco, CA 94133
citylights.com

CONTENTS

Foreword

JUSTIN TORRES

I DID NOT KNOW Gil Cuadros in the flesh, never heard his voice, nor shook his hand, nor did I take him to bed (alas). I met him after death, through the single book he published in his lifetime, *City of God*. I remember the book was pressed into my hands by an old friend, the poet and scholar Jaime Shearn Coan, who had lost a loved one to AIDS, and whose own critical and creative work focused on the artistic and personal legacies of the epidemic. "You need to read this book," he said. "It's going to blow your mind." It did. Cuadros was the writer I'd been waiting for, a voice from the recent past, that missing generation ravaged by plague. I studied his text like holy scripture, lured in by his ghostly presence on the page, and with each rereading I felt him resurrected; I understood how much had been lost.

Cuadros knew how to write about marginalization—or as my colleague, Rafael Pérez-Torres, once wisely put it, Cuadros knew about "the body doubly marked." Latino, born and raised in East Los Angeles, Cuadros plumbs desire—childhood fantasies, adult lust. He navigates both Chicano Southern California and that other, gay, Los Angeles, largely white. For me, his writing has incredible personal resonance; he is brilliant about family, God, sex, racism, homophobia in the community, white lovers, violence. The writing is haunting and revelatory. As I've written elsewhere, Cuadros admired and understood Genet—which is to say he knew about the shock and poetry of honestly putting into words what we perverts do with our bodies, and what we only wish we could do.

I've been reading *City of God* for two decades now, learning from the urgency of the prose, teaching the book year after year. It never stales. For a book whose making was conditioned by the author's impending death, *City of God* is radiant and startlingly alive. Each rereading, each new class discussion, like the turning of a prism, offers up some brilliant and unexpected refraction, though inevitably, when I close the book, I'm left with the desire for more. I want to stay inside his words, his rhythms, his life. Here is the beginning of a brilliant literary voice, and at the same time, his work is also about the silencing and strangulation of that voice. Not just by AIDS, not just by illness and death, but by everything AIDS connotes in the context of the 1980s and early '90s—social and governmental indifference to queer suffering, inflamed machismo, churchly condemnation, racial disparity, weekly funerals. How maddening, how tragic, to know that Cuadros was dead at age thirty-four.

When I learned of *My Body Is Paper*—the book you hold in your hands—a manuscript of Cuadros's uncollected writings pieced together from his archives and brought out some thirty years after the publication of *City of God*, I felt a kind of ecstasy akin to the convert's anticipation of the second coming. This was quickly followed by apprehension. What if the previously unpublished work failed to live up to the power of Cuadros's debut, or worse, diluted the magnificence of that book? (I shudder to think about anyone glimpsing my own early drafts—I'm a writer who believes not everything composed in the dark need come to light.) How could the newly discovered work ever be as limpid and burnished and deep and layered as the stories and poems that make up his first book?

I needn't have worried. All Cuadros's gifts and obsessions are on full, radiant display in *My Body Is Paper*. Here are the familiar archetypes Cuadros creates out of family and lovers. Here is the ornate religious symbolism. Here are the cocks, the focus on pleasure and self-pleasure, a finger up the butt. Here is the omnipresence of the father, who seems to be forever climbing into bed with his young son after a fight with the mother, at times a monster in the dark, other times musk and muscle and cuddles. Here the troubled eminence of the queer child—that little brown boy lighting himself on fire, or nearly getting himself drowned. Here is West Hollywood. Here are the bars and the camp icons—Marlene, Audrey, Tallulah. Here is East Los Angeles. Here is the Latino face whose only tongue is English, and the rural cousins, darker, who have Spanish. Here are the descriptions of illness and drug-related psychosis. Here are visions, premonitions, visitations, ghosts. Here is mother on the phone, swearing, *It's like you killed me*. Here are the lovers in the garden, dirt underneath their nails. Here are the lovers who meld one into the other. Here are the masters and here is willful submission and here is defiance. Here is the old issue of the *New Yorker* in the waiting room with the poem about a pear (was it Updike? "Pear like a Potato"? *It wanted to grow, and it did. It / had a shape in mind, and if that shape in transit / was waylaid by scars, by cells / too mean to join in . . . well, it kept on going / anyway . . .*). Here are the poems and lessons and suffering and illness and grace that make the poet. Here is Gil, always Gil, uncompromised and uncompromising, and without doubt one of the sexiest and most important writers I've ever read.

The title, *My Body Is Paper*, is taken from the opening stanza of the poem "If She Could." The speaker is talking about his mother who, like a pair of scissors, would cut out the faggy parts, as well as the illness, from her son's paper body. Beyond that sense of paper, of course, there is the literary sense of a corpus, a body of work. Also, the sense of deterioration, the paper-thin skin of the very ill. The body made paper reminds me, too, of the parchment of holy books, animal skins scraped, burnished, and stitched together—and because I come from a long line of Catholics, I think of the paper-thin communion wafer, the consumable body, forever ingestible and forever reproducible. That is, when I read *My Body Is Paper*, I am reminded of the concept of mystical recurrence. *Take this paper and read it, this is his body, broken for us. Do this in remembrance of Gil.*

MY BODY IS PAPER

I

I have no hands but yours.

HANDS

I AM PREPARED. I have had my will drawn and notarized. I've given away old books from my library that I will never read again. I've gotten rid of porno magazines and cock rings, things that would be difficult or compromising for my beloved to discard. Mother has all my baby pictures I stole. I have paid for my cremation. I carry a pocket full of change to give to panhandlers. My elementary Catechism has returned; *those who help the lowliest . . .*

Marcus says he just doesn't understand me sometimes, says he has dreams for us, a home we will build together, but it seems to him I'm giving parts of my life away. I sit quietly at the deli booth, staring at my unfinished sandwich. It is rare now for me to be hungry; the bones in my face have become more distinct. It is when I don't respond that he gets annoyed, but I can't help it. I don't want to change his feelings or argue the probabilities. I don't believe I have long; my blood has turned against me, there is no one here to heal me. The sunlight from the window poured heavily onto his face, rugged and aged. Myself, I have to stay away from the sun; my face discolors from all the medications I take.

Marcus has become quiet, maybe brooding. I hear a knock on the window next to me. It is a tall man, very dark and in a ragged black suit. He points with a dirty finger at the tray that holds my half-eaten sandwich, then brings his fingers to his mouth. I nod my head. Marcus hates when I do stuff like that, and he barks, "Why'd you do that? Why can't you just save it for later?"

The man comes to our table, pulls the tray closer to him, unwraps the sandwich from the paper. Marcus leans back far away. The man is intimidating, his form towers over us. I want to tell him to take it away; but he just stands there and eats. Finally, Marcus says, "There's an empty table over there!" The man gives thanks and then asks for the rest of my drink, which I refuse because I know it would piss Marcus off, since he bought lunch. Marcus and I are silent for the rest of his lunch break.

It has become a ritual of sorts, to have lunch on Thursday with Marcus at his work. Sometimes I am too early, or I can see that he is busy with a client. The nursery is very dense and serene, and as he walks through it, he is in total command, like a god in his Eden. The customers are rapt at his every word on how to take care of the plant, what it is suited for, what it will look like in a year, two years. This is one of the reasons I love him, his ability to nurture. It is like he knows the secrets of life and wants to share them with me. I don't want to be seen at his work. This is a way I show him my love. My face looks too haggard. I have strange discolorations on my forehead and chest. I look as if I am going to die soon. I don't want any rumors started about Marcus and me at his work. I don't want him having to answer difficult questions about his *friend*. I can imagine his soiled hands clenching.

When I am early, or he's busy, I go sit at this small Catholic church across the street. The parking lot is usually empty, and there's a porch by the rectory, which I go sit on. The Father has looked at me before through his window and knows that I am just there to wait.

Often when I am there, a large Mexican woman comes by. She carries paper bags from Pic 'n' Save. Over the brims of the bags, plastic and silk flowers stick out. Some weeks they are all blue, others purple, still other times pink and red. The woman has taken to nodding at me, "Como 'sta?"

One day, with a smile on my face, I said, "Merci." She gave me a look and then I knew I'd made a mistake, "Bien, bien, Señora!"

She laughed and said, "Ay."

French has always come easier to me. I'm sure she thinks I'm some sort of "pocho," like an Oreo, brown on the outside, white on the inside.

The large woman usually wears something that my grandmother would wear, a kind of flowery smock so she won't get dirty. She decorates the statue of Mary that stands in the corner of the parking lot, under a large, sturdy eucalyptus tree. On holidays, she's put plastic jack-o'-lanterns, Styrofoam snowmen at Mary's feet, and always lots and lots of fake flowers. Marcus has often told me that he'd give me some perennials, other flowering plants to give to the woman, but I think she wouldn't want them. I think she loves the fake flowers' everlasting quality. She does it as a devotion, and when she finishes, she prays, her knees on the cement, her head bowed down, hands pressed together. I've told Marcus it is like she has her own form of serenity, that she sees beauty over life, or that she sees her actions as more important than presenting living things.

The most notable thing about the Mary statue is that she has no hands.

Being at the rectory alone makes me think of death. Would I do it to myself if I got really ill? What if I start losing my mind? What if I start looking like more of a freak than I already do and people start staring? What if it becomes too painful for Marcus to be with me?

My upbringing haunts me, like a shadow of the tree. I was taught that I could never go to heaven if I killed myself, even the most ill cannot do that, because life is a gift we must fully use or otherwise appear ungrateful. My archbishop taught me that. My parents had set up those meetings with Archbishop Mahoney because they didn't know what to do with me, and they were afraid a doctor would lock me up in an institution. When I was twelve, I had already tried pills I got at school and from my father's medicine cabinet. The paramedic who revived me cried openly, said he'd never seen a young boy try such a thing. Worse yet, my parents were horrified when they came out to the garage and saw lit stacks of newspaper, soaked with lighter fluid, surrounding me. Parts of my arms and legs were burned severely, and today I carry those scars. No one ever understood why I would become so quiet, disappear into my parents' closet for hours in the dark. Sometimes I would torture my pets, make the other children on our block cry. Still the only feeling I have now is guilt, and when I think of myself, I think I've wasted my life. All I remember fully though is a sound, the rush of air igniting.

I figured the hands of Mary must have broken off during an earthquake, or maybe due to vandals. There's a bronze plaque that reads, "I have no hands, but yours."

The day I read that, the Mexican woman had come up behind me quietly and placed her hand on my shoulder. She started speaking Spanish much too quickly for me to understand, when she figured out I didn't speak Spanish well enough, she switched over to a slow English. "My name es Yoli, Yolanda."

It was my turn to say, "Como 'sta?"

There was a gentleness in her voice. "I see you here all the time." I told her I was waiting for a friend. "Oh, you can help me though?" She pulled out a small hand rake and said, "Weeds."

I got onto my knees with a chuckle and started raking out the weeds that had grown in the flower bed. Eventually, my hands began to ache from the exertion. It was very quiet work.

She changed the vases and put blue flowers and then some calla lilies in the glass containers. I told her how Marcus worked at the nursery across the street and said that I could give her some flowers and other plants if she wanted. I told her maybe some small ivy around the edges would be nice. She smiled and said, "Gracias."

I started to notice the meditative quality of working this soil, how there was something like a warm charge I received from the earth, that I became more spirit than being. And like the wind flittering through the eucalyptus tree, it felt like she was speaking to me telepathically.

"My son used to do this every Thursday, before I took over." I stopped what I was doing. "He loved real plants, fussed over this small garden. The Father mentioned often how devoted Tulio was, how his love was an example to all of us. I was so proud of him." On Yoli's face, I saw a pride I wished my own parents could give me. "The women of the church would surround me and praise me for raising such a fine young man. But nobody saw how lonely he was. How he would drink in my kitchen till he passed out crying, 'Mama, Mama.'"

I turned back to my work, flustered because I knew how he needed to create beauty in his life. "When the earthquake came," she said, "and the hands of Mary broke, he wanted the church to have it fixed, but Father said, 'No, it is more symbolic this way.' Tulio could not understand; it was like the Mother of God was a real person to him and needed to be healed."

I huffed, thinking of my own life. She turned her face away from me. "Everyone was surprised that day. I wasn't. They came to my house, the Father, women of the church. I could tell they had been crying. They said, 'Yoli, don't cry but you have to see your son, you have to come with us.' Tulio had said he was going to trim down the tree over Mary, that the boughs were too low, so off he went with the ladder and some rope."

The shade of the tree covered us both as she spoke. "Mary stands so far away from the street no one noticed Tulio stringing up the rope, pushing himself off the ladder. When I saw him, it seemed the air gently rocked him back and forth, his feet nearly touched the head of Mary. It was many days before I cried; somehow, I knew it was all my fault."

I wanted to ask her why, but I knew. Tulio saw no life ahead, and simply creating these altars was not enough. He was a man who wanted to heal and to be healed.

Marcus came at that moment, asked me to see a ficus tree he wanted to bring home. All I could say to Yoli was, "I'm sorry, so sorry." Marcus was proud of the ficus he had picked for me; it looked sturdy, the roots unbound. Near the trees were shelves with pots and ceramic figures of cherubs and gargoyles. I noticed that a few of the cherubs' arms were broken, parts of the wings missing. I could see myself grinding the arms down just to the hands and I started contemplating whether I should use glue or plaster, maybe cement.

I couldn't tell if it was an act of creation or violence against the church. Maybe both. In my mind I saw what Tulio must have looked like. His smile must have been dazzling.

I picked up the broken arm and asked Marcus if I could possibly have this and another hand. Marcus shrugged his shoulders, questioned me, Do I want the tree or what? I kissed him lightly on the mouth, surrounded by the lushness of the nursery. He looked embarrassed in his paradise.

FATHER FIGURE

I'd always been attracted to the type of men
my mother loathed,
the hairy back,
thick-chested,
foul-mouthed bastards
whose cocks endlessly protruded
from the hole in their cotton briefs.
They would poke it between her legs
while she slept against them like a spoon.

I was a light sleeper
and would wake at any bump
or dream.
Once there was a man
standing at my bedroom door.
He was dark next to my chalkboard
with the alphabet trim.
I thought he was my dad
and asked him what he wanted.
He stood like a silhouette
slightly thinner than my father,
a bit taller than five-four.
I brought the blanket closer to my chin,
whispered, "Dad?"
My parents thought it was a nightmare

but they checked the doors and windows
and only the side gate was closed.
My father walked around in his yellowed jockeys
hanging loose at the crotch and ass.
My mother kept yelling at him,
"Put some pants on!"
She clutched tightly to the open lace
at her throat.
Her arms were crossed to protect her breast.
I told her, "I could have touched him."

My father had dreams
of opening his own construction company.
At the age of twelve,
I knew plumbing, carpentry, electrical wiring,
and landscaping. I could add cabinets,
take out walls, mix paint, drop ceilings,
insulate, fit pipe, and lay tile.
I was his first boy.
My father would turn my hands
palms to the sky
checking for calluses.
He'd show me his
and say, "These are the hands of a man."

ARDENT LETTERS

I.

We make fires in the hills circled in stones
aluminum cans, carry matches in our backpacks,
hidden between schoolbooks and sheaves of paper,
our bags slung low down our spines.
Joel is growing silent as I always have been,
broods in the last row in class, stays to himself.
He's written letters about how he'll miss me,
two grades his senior and I entering high school.
Joel scrambles over the fence in the road,
where broken asphalt crumbles into wash.
We pass the remains of other sacrifices,
blackened earth, marks against the land.

A sign states: Keep out, unsafe.
Past the gated boundary, wind steers
through branches, whittles the underbrush.
His red-banded socks attract the tiny barbs
of dry weeds that prick ankles.
My palms become stained with tree sap,
the limbs we use as ropes to ascend the hill.
Joel applies his spit to rub my hands clean.
Into the fires we throw the poems
written to each other, couplets that rhyme.
Lines then words curl into ash;

and we say always this will be the last.

We sit where we can see the whole city,
doleful skyscrapers thrust above smog.
Joel stokes the blaze with a twisted branch,
lays his head on my shoulder, hair falls in a sweep
to cover his mouth. I turn my attention
along the horizon, can see several crosses
jutting off spires, steeples in gold.
I feel Joel's breath swirl down my shirt,
smell the eucalyptus leaves nesting in the fire.
The scent is that of a church, a sermon that burns
the pulpit, tightens my lungs. Our hand-written letters
transmute into smoke, linger in the clothes we've worn all day.

2.
My father is a monster
in the darkness of my bedroom.
The stretch of his white T-shirt, chest heaving,
looks as if something is about to tear.
He holds a sheet of paper, shakes it like a rattle,
a voodoo doctor, expelling demons from his son.
I recognize the letter, had found it hidden between books
left on my desk, the whole class in conspiracy.
I had folded it several times, trying to make it disappear
till it was nothing but a mark inside my palm.
My father's machinist hand shoves it open in my face,
all I see are diamond creases, words that make me flush and burn.

Pete sat in the last row in 9th grade, typing
near me and the other bad typist,
all in order, the best to worst, fastest to slowest.
He continually pressed his knee into my leg,

tried to get my attention while
Coach Melvin lectured on the J and F keys.
I pushed his thigh aside with my hand,
his face always with a sly smile.
During practice, he typed out letters to me
addressed from Hadagee, the Armenian student,
fat and hairy who wore sweaters too small,
high-water pants, smelled of cabbage, couldn't speak English.

Pete wrote how Hadagee wanted to see me sprawled
on his bed, how good it would feel
to have me suck his dick, lick his balls.
Once, he wrote how I'll feel like a real woman,
humped by him on all fours, moaning for
what makes him a real man. He signed with his own name,
a mistake, he claimed, when I shoved it back in his face.
My father wants Pete taken out of school,
transferred to a program for troubled students.
Pete sits across from me in the principal's office, red-faced,
a wooden paddle above his head, whispers he's gonna get me.
Inside myself, something burns down my thigh, warm as piss.

3.
I see Joel in the halls, he returns my stares with hate,
the kind of disgust my father holds in his eyes. In the garage
I write on the back pages of an astronomy book, cryptic
letters and plans, how to make my father's car explode.
When I was seven, I wrote with his cologne,
spilled Roman Brio on the oil-stained garage floor,
letters, patterns, symbols taken from the zodiac.
With a match stolen off the stove, I'd light the tail end,
watch the shimmer of blue flames race through its design
only to perish meekly, a tongue lapping at the final bit of air,

as if tasting the hand of its maker. What remained—
my father's scent enclosed in his pitch-black workspace.

Here's the only letter I'm not afraid he'll find and read:
Dear Dad,
I know you don't love me.
The time I drowned in that cold algae lake you made me swim,
my feet bound in fishing line, and you wouldn't get your clothes wet,
wouldn't jump in like a cannonball to save me, or touch
your mouth against mine. Some other man breathed into me.
I remember how I always kissed you goodnight, forehead and chin,
the sides of your cheeks, in the sign of the cross, as if this son's
devotion was holy as church. I used to think love was baseball bats,
pieces of sawed-off wood, belts, and fists in the warm gaseous
toolshed where you struck the back of my legs like flint.

When I come to the letter's end,
I don't know how to finish, so I pile
newspapers into a corner, make a small closet
I can sit comfortably inside, knees to chest.
It reminds me of confession, purgatory
moments before Father would slide open the window,
his mouth obscured, describing the penance
I must perform. I spray the newspaper
with lighter fluid, the sheets becoming dark
as if pissed on, the odor shrouds, incense
or cologne. It takes less than a second,
flames shoot up the walls, around my feet, calves singed.

I bite my lips not to cry,
hear my father's taunts to keep
my eyes on his pitched baseball.

I step out of the inferno,
fight fire with splashes of water,
the walls blackened to the ceiling.
Dad, I am the sissy-boy
you never wanted, afraid you'll find
what wasn't burnt, the blisters
along my legs, smell the ignited fuel.
Pieces of ash flit in the air, land
in my hair, mark me gray and pungent.

ERIC

I'VE KNOWN ERIC for some time now; we really grew up together, ran the streets, did school, smoked dope behind his fat-assed mother's house. Eric didn't even live with his mother; he stayed over at his sister's because he couldn't handle the way his mother hounded him, always sticking her nose in his business.

I had been over the one time that Eric lashed back at her because she'd been checking his sheets, seeing if they'd been tucked in right or if he was hiding something. It'd been building up for some time; I could tell by the way she said hello to me when I came to walk with Eric to school. If it was a good morning, she'd be drinking coffee, smoking a cigarette in front of *Good Morning America*. If it was a bad morning, she'd be dusting, complaining no one ever helped her out and stuff.

This morning when Eric let me in the door, the living room was filled with piles of clothes, freshly washed; even Eric smelled of detergent. When we were about to leave, his mother started yelling to get back here; she'd been in his room, had ripped the covers off the bed and wanted him to do his bed all over again. She kept on yelling, "Why can't you do this right, you're just in my way, can't wait till I can kick you out of my house."

Eric had been saying what a wack his mom was being, tearing the place apart. The day before, she'd grabbed him by the collar and pushed him out of the house because he'd left a towel on the bathroom floor. His mother was hard-faced, right up next to Eric's, nearly spitting words at him. I guess Eric snapped because he just shoved her

16

hard against the wall. She wanted to strike him, but he held her fist in his hand and then tossed it back to her. She started screaming some more, "I'm going to kill you, god dammit!" I grabbed Eric by the arm, his white T-shirt twisted in my fingers as I tore him out of the house, nearly ripping the screen door off its hinges.

. Eric hid in my garage while his mother's boyfriend went looking for him. My parents didn't give a shit. "No motherfucker is going to be messing in our backyard!" My father's voice shook as he asked, "Do you want me to get my gun, or would you like to get your ugly face away from my garage?" What a joke, but you got to love my dad; he didn't own a gun because my mother would have harped on him forever.

They had always left me alone with Eric. Actually, my parents liked him. Eric did have a cleanliness about him, hair cropped short, a twenty on him at all times, in his wallet's secret slot, folded, moist and accordioned.

We hung behind the steam plant, next to the hill and his apartment. He waited for me to come by, squatting on the brick wall that held the ivy lawn back, next to the pay phone where he had called me over. As a greeting I brushed my hand discreetly along his inner thigh, disturbing the perfect curls of hair on his body, fed my fingers down, inside the crotch of his loose cotton shorts, till they swam in his humidity. For the rest of the day, I'd be conscious of him, his odor distinct and comforting under my nails.

Eric and I would watch the columns of steam being pumped out of the electrical plant. There was a mattress flung out in the nearby dried grass. We would rest on it, the material warm from the sun, and listen to the water rushing down slatted wood, a part of the process to give the city energy. We'd talk long stuff, like did we believe in God or whatever. I told him I couldn't; it was kind of pointless. I couldn't possibly know any of his intentions, so why worry if he knows you believe in him or not. Eric sort of hated these discussions I'd bring up; he was more interested in getting out of this hellhole he was living in, and if

I would go away with him. We'd finish a lunch, large bottles of Cokes. Sometimes Eric would pull out his dick and take a piss on an old, withered oak. Sometimes I could see it splash till the last few drops fell. He'd turn to me and stuff it back in.

The street over, I had a job at Bobby's Liquor on Fair Oaks. I lied about my age; they never checked. I took the late shift, worked minimum; it paid minimum. Eric and I spent the money going to clubs and shit. I swept floors, pinned up posters of Dos Equis women, a beer bottle in one hand, a two-fingered tequila in the other.

I'm half Mexican. My mother grew up here; she looked pretty. Her sisters would call her güera, making sure she never felt good about being so pale. They made jokes about me before I was born, wondering what I'd look like because my mother's boyfriend was white. When my mother turned thirty, I was already fourteen. I was watching a video while she argued on the phone with her older sister, saying, "You've got to respect me, you can't treat me like a dog. I don't want to hear from you again."

I never got on my mother's bad side either because she could drop you like that. She always acted like I was delivering bad news to her if I mentioned anything, would grab her lungs, relieved that the problem was minuscule, unimportant. She was a good lady, though, died of cancer a few years back.

My father got into AA, best thing for him. He doesn't like me working at Bobby's, but fuck it, I'm not, as he says, codependent. Sometimes he waits for me parked in front of the store so I don't have to take the bus at night. When I open the passenger door, he says, "Hi." His breath smells of coffee; I know he's wired.

I tell him, "Let's go out for dinner." We drive up the street to the Salt Shaker, let the little old ladies serve us. He orders his steak and eggs. I don't really want to eat, but he gets lonely after his meetings, tells me I really should go with him.

The year my mother died, Eric hung out at our place. His sister didn't want him much either; he was seventeen, could join the army or get a good job. One time, my father wanted to go after Eric's throat. Dad worked nights, molded plastics. One morning, Eric and I were at the kitchen table, breakfast almost finished; we were half-dressed for school. Eric sat there on the dinette chair, turned away from the table, shirtless, jeans on, the fly still unbuttoned. He slipped on one white cotton sock, then the other. I sat watching him, his legs opening then closing, slowly eating my maple syrup pancakes, my eyes focused on his every move, sinews twisted, then the sudden glint of his smile my way. I was near naked, just my white jockeys when my dad stepped in. He took one look at me, one at Eric. I could feel his thoughts right where they say the soul is, a feeling that yelled, 'Why are you taking the one thing I have left in my life?'

My father tried to act natural, tried to take a series of deep breaths, looking at the stacks of letters he had already opened, the magazine on the TV set, glaring at Eric lacing his shoes, pulling the striped bands tight. Eventually, my father walked into his bedroom, slammed the door, put on the cheap portable he bought off someone at work, wailed a tape of Lyle Lovett. It was a tape my mother had. She played it a lot after she lost her sight.

I had gone to the hospital every day, before and after school. We didn't talk much. She stayed in her bed, sick from chemo. I would try some homework, read a magazine. I don't remember the exact moment when my father and I found out she was going to die; we just knew. Once I came into her room; bandages wrapped her eyes and there was a sharp smell of her body, the room lit by a low-cloud day. A nurse walked in ready to soap my mother down; she left when she saw me. Sometimes my mother would know I had walked in, other times she didn't know who I was. She'd ask for me over and over, and I'd say, "I'm here. Mom, I'm here." I'd try to hold her hand, but she wouldn't let me; she wouldn't turn her head toward me. She kept on slipping her hand out of mine till my father would grab me from behind, pulling me away, kissing the top of my head, suffocating me in his arms, saying, "my baby, my sweet baby." I would hit at him, my face on his chest, his arms locked around me, the heat of his body useless and unwanted.

I told Eric, "Even now I can feel her inside my hand." He'd try to change the subject on our long drives at night in his sister's beat-up old Cougar. His sister would lend it to him if she knew he was coming over to visit me. When I called Eric and she answered, she'd always ask about my mother. I guess she felt sorry for me.

There was a park above Foothill; a small wooden amphitheater was built on the incline. Eric and I would sit staring at all the lights in the valley, like an electrical grid. He'd pull a joint out and we'd get stoned. I would try to tell him what it was like, but he'd say, "Don't dwell on it; it'll just be worse if you do." My chest and throat would burn, and I'd space out on the trees, where a sudden ember flared, a man smoking a cigarette, looking at Eric and me as if we were bones to suck on. Back in the car, I was more comfortable, slipping my hand along Eric's chest, underneath his soft brown leather jacket, the silk lining, the pocket of his cotton T-shirt. My hand slipped inside the pocket, as his mouth opened and moved toward mine.

My mother passed away in the hospital when my father and I weren't around. The late-night phone call of the doctor made her death real, made the walls shake, my father throwing himself against the doors of their bedroom. I tried to stay asleep, tried to pick up a dream where I left it, downtown L.A. at night, men ratty from the street, following Eric and me. I wanted to set the dream's outcome right, to not let them throw empty beer bottles at us, the glass breaking on our heads, my father breaking open the door of my bedroom, saying, "You have to get up, baby, I have something to tell you."

That night I called Eric, told him my mother had died. He came over right away. My father was out somewhere drinking. Eric brought a couple of six-packs from his brother-in-law's cooler. We watched the news from my bed, our legs crossed over each other identically, Eric handing me cold beer after cold beer, till my stomach was ice. The local channels were talking about how the police were still looking for two men, last seen in another area of town, a bike trail near an elementary school, a fourteen-year-old murdered.

Eric shut off the TV, started pulling off my shirt, rubbed the insides of my arms, his palms dry against my skin. He folded each article of clothing with care, followed pleats and collars, placed them on the long wooden-backed chair hooked under the door. He was already shirtless and, as he started loosening his belt, the metal buckle picked up reflections of my room, my face on the bed, my look that this will solve everything, that I can lose myself here, that I can't let my mother rule my life. When he pushed his dick up inside me, as far as it would go, I turned my head away, saw an image burned into the TV set, a young face, a school picture, could hear a car going down my street, a wail, a song, and Eric whispering with warm breath, like steam, "Everything will be all right," his hands trying to hold onto mine and I won't let him.

II

*If she could, she would cut out
what is wrong with me.*

TRADITION

My father takes over her territory,
always clean, scented with pine
and lemon dish soap, the daily meals
constantly emerge swathed in steam
and sweet pea–embroidered linens.
Her kitchen table becomes his workbench
covered with large tin pots and Tupperware,
the timeworn AM radio plays Christmas oldies
spun by Art Laboe and Casey Kasem.
The stove simmers with meat sauce,
splatters the white porcelain of the Amana.
He marks the counters where he lays
the juicy red spoon. Mother wants to hover,
sponge in hand, while my father
shows me this fine art of tradition.
His brawny calloused hands guide me
as I spread the ground cornmeal
across the ridged surfaces of husks
still wet from a water-filled pan.
The tarnished butter knife reflects our faces,
his dissatisfaction at my poor mockery of a tamale.
He thumps his own knife against the bowl
shakes off the excess, speaks of his father
and uncles all gone into Jesus' heaven
who watch down on us in sweat-stained T-shirts

to see if we do it the way they would,
always ready to belch a criticism, to say
it's been spread on too thick, too thin
our tamales are not as good,
that somehow we fail.

"CHARGE"

Dad's *Herald* is spread open;
it fans the floor, thrown down
like a Persian wall to wall.
My mother presses her favorite new skirt,
a simple dress that fits her well,
slims her hips.
He can see through sheer cloth
as it unpleats from the board.
She sprinkles the dress,
the smell of steam lingers.

He can taste it too.
He has lined up three Millers
and stretches for the radio.
She stops for a moment
to hear a whirl of sounds run by
till pre-game Dodger talk is on.
Willie Mays is her hero Giant,
a fury from center-field mythology,
whose swing can rip the skin
off anyone. Dad argues,
"The guy's a bum!"
But still she's learned the sport,
loves to see him all worked up, veins bulge,
as if he could go down to the field,

compare his biceps next to Mays's.
Dad's half-talking to her,
half-talking to the RCA, wavering,
its antenna reaching over the hill
that blocks the stadium's signal
from our house.

She finishes the hem
and stands in the full-length mirror
surrounded by myrtle garlands,
brass rose buttons.
The dress rubs against her,
embroidered with seductive powers.
She swings with short steps,
small pelvic motions.

Dad coaches behind bottle glasses,
tiny diamond shapes hinged to his frames.
He drinks his beer
lets foam stay on his mustache.
His lips are wet and cold.

She leaves him to put her skirt away,
on a clip hanger from the dry cleaners.
The paper is still on the wire,
the game is about to start.

MY FATHER'S SNORING IS WILD TONIGHT

My mother hates this intrusive noise;
She pushes him out with foot and claw,
covers her cold cream face with a goose
down pillow, folds and gathers her flannel nightgown
between cameo legs. She shudders and dissolves
into a pre-embryo state. I am dreaming

that it is I who pulls the milkweeds and
dandelions for Dad; it is I who bends over
the flower bed, my hand fisted deep inside
with wet fingers latched around the main root.
The thick, wild mustard breaks while he comes
to slumber in my twin and rolls me out.

She yells, "Close that door, let me sleep
in peace!" Now, I am cupped into my father's body
with the smell of arms and forty-weight oil.
His hairy legs settle on my smooth ankles,
and the blanket wraps us in crochet knots,
cotton briefs, and his large, white T-shirt.

SHE PICKED THEM UP IN MEXICO

the fisted arm,
the open eye
the thick metal lungs,
medallions made to heal,
three for a dollar.

and it was the lungs
that were between her breasts.
when twisted around
it looked more like a double-headed axe
than how anyone could breathe.

and she would have to remind herself
to breathe,
when she was mad,
when Rupert came up from behind
wanting to be let in,
or when in the morning he left,
saying he didn't want to wake her.

and it wasn't until
the chain broke,
slipping out of her blouse,
that she began to wear the open eye
and the fisted arm,
more voluminous,
and lighter weight.

COMING OUT

*(October 11, 1991: National Coming Out Day. My boyfriend is in
Sacramento protesting the veto of AB101, after the California governor cam-
paigned he'd sign a bill to protect lesbians and gays from job discrimination.)*

When my mother said, "Why are you trying to drive me to death?"
I remembered the kind of car we had in Driver's Ed,
two large wheels on the dash, two speedometers,
two sets of brakes. The homely instructor
smelled of body odor, polyester, a low-paid academic, hairy.
He led me to believe I was the one in control.
maneuvering through traffic, city-born to drive.
When I went too fast, the needle at 35, he'd slow me down,
grab the steering as I made a corner. "Left on Garfield,
not Albright." He'd ask me to pull over,
use the example of other students' abilities to yield,
to merge smoothly behind the car in front of them,
as if speed or talent to find alternative routes weren't necessary.
The instructor would say, "Driving is a privilege, not a right."
I knew I'd get my temporary permit anyway,
had always done well on written exams, could quote the ratio
of acceleration and stopping, how many deaths per year
were caused by driving under stress.
I tried to calm my mother,
as if to tell her, "See, Mom, here's what I look like,
name, address, weight, color of hair,
laminated, all perfectly normal,
the word 'license' emblazoned on the top,
the state seal golden, a grizzly, an Amazon,
the motto Eureka."

CIGAR CIGAR

THE BOYS ON our block called Carlos "Cigar" because of the buzz haircut his parents made him get every other Sunday at El Cid's barbers in the Food City shopping center. It was a perfect flat-top, no longer than an inch on top, bare skin around the ears, strange for the time—Robert Kennedy's assassination; most boys were growing their hair long. When Sirhan Sirhan was convicted we started calling Cigar, "Cigar Cigar," giving him an exotic fearsomeness his short, stubby body lacked otherwise. I had a long wiry mess of hair, and my parents admired Cigar's more boyish, military look, creased khakis, polished black shoes, fists thrust down to his crotch like a flexing bodybuilder. My father would rub the top of Cigar's head as if rubbing for luck, as if wishing I would be more like Cigar, or that Cigar was his own boy.

Cigar wasn't all Mexican like the other boys on our street. Even Victor, who was Japanese and went to Japanese school, looked more like us with his dark skin and black hair than Cigar did. He had brownish hair, pale skin with freckles, greenish eyes. His mother was naturally blond, unlike our mothers who dyed their hair that color in streaks. Cigar's mother was our Cub Scout den mother and didn't appreciate Cigar Cigar's nickname. She asked us seriously as we sat in a Cub Scout meeting circle how we would feel if we were called a bad name. Victor pushed his shoulder into mine and I shoved back and Cigar started shoving into me also and soon we were all giggling. Cigar's mother wondered, "What's so funny?" and Victor said he knew a bad word, and Cigar started laughing again, telling me to say it. Cigar's mother tapped her foot, said she didn't know if she wanted to know what that word was. Cigar punched me in the arm, and I yelled out, "You stupid wetback!"

Cigar's mother gasped loudly, her face turning red. She reached down and grabbed my arm. She kept on stuttering, "I can't believe . . . Wait till . . . Where did you. . . ." Cigar's mother ushered me through her house. Cigar's father sat reading a newspaper, and she told him she had to take this boy home, that he said a bad word. Cigar's father worked at a military base; a mechanic, he and my father would sometimes help each other fix their cars, drinking underneath the open hoods, giving advice. I could always see their heads down in an engine, their brown Mexican arms streaked with grease, hands reaching for some tool. His wife whispered the word into his ear and he just grinned wildly, shaking his head as if told a dull joke.

As Cigar's mother and I neared my home, her hand still gripped around my arm, I told her I heard the word all the time. I said, "The truck drivers coming off the freeway yell it out their windows as we're walking to school. My mother yells it at all the crazy drivers on the road, all the time."

This seemed to make Cigar's mother loosen her hold on my arm. She looked down at me, less angry. "Well, I still should say something to your mother." My mother was pulling her car out of the driveway and saw us coming up the sidewalk. Cigar's mother leaned into the window and said to my mother, "Your son said a bad word so he can't stay for the meeting."

My mother sighed audibly. "Get in the car," she huffed at me and thanked Cigar's mother.

Cigar's mother said, "Don't you want to know what he said?" My mother shook her head. "I can already imagine."

Years later, Cigar and I both joined the high school Explorer Scouts. It was a vocational training program with courses in law enforcement, small business, and accounting. Cigar and I had a mutual interest in photography, and the Explorers allowed us to use the photo lab late after the school closed and before adult classes started. We had both become staff photographers for the school annual and newspaper. The editors could always count on Cigar and me to be at a game, to have a close-up of the game's MVP and the winning touchdown, basket, or run. We'd also get special requests: student council members or alumni in the front row of the bleachers, a certain cheerleader doing a cheer with her dress hiked up. Cigar and I were very popular with the team members. Between classes, we'd spread out black-and-white proof sheets on lunch tables, the football team huddled around us, taking orders for 3x5s, 5x7s, and 8x10s, sometimes even 16x20s. Cigar saved up enough money to buy a souped-up Cougar; I used our earned money for food and clothes. Even the coaches gave Cigar and me special treatment. Due to the passage of Proposition 13, the Howard Jarvis taxpayers' revolt bill, school budgets went dry, and the entire social studies department was taken over by physical ed. All I had to do to get out of California History was tell Coach Melvin that I had "pics" from the game last night. Coach would open his roll book, mark near my name, and it would be like I'd stayed for the entire class.

On away games, after the last whistle was blown, Cigar and I would be drawn into the locker rooms as if we were team players, being rough-housed, towels snapping at our asses, our heads vise-gripped underneath sweaty arms, being passed along from player to player. It was a time of dirty talk, of kicking ass, showing what pussies the other guys were, making them suck our dicks. Everyone around me seemed to move in slow motion, like I was on acid or cocaine, the smell of their sweat, the mold on the tile entering through my nose. Glimpses of bare bodies moving into showers, asses and cocks, all the different shapes, bulbous helmets and cherries underneath folds of foreskin, jockstraps and tube socks lying on the cement floor, bare feet splashing puddles of water.

The only requirement the Explorers made for the year was a portfolio. The portfolio needed to consist of several types of photography—commercial still life, portrait, wedding, journalism, and fashion. Even though I made my money with sports journalism, I was strangely drawn to fashion. I'd pore over *Vogue, Elle, Mademoiselle*, studying the provocative poses, the suggestions of sexual encounters on the street, violence, and abandonment. My favorite photos required an acrylic body harness over bare skin, a woman riding a saddle on a Queen Anne chair, or a real mannequin in a group of similarly dressed real women. Once a week, I'd ask some pretty light-skinned girl who looked like one of the models to pose for me. She would be flattered. She'd ask, disbelieving, if she would make a good model. I'd show her the page with the model I thought she looked like. The girl would stare at the page, as if disassembling the model to see what parts really were needed to make her. Finally, the girl would say something like, "If I pulled my hair back this way, if I wore that style of makeup, I could look like her."

The Explorers always took a final trip for the school year. This year we were going to Death Valley to photograph the dunes and desert scenery, Devil's Golf Course, the sherbet-colored mountains. Cigar had been putting off his assignments, doing more and more sports photos to keep up with the costs of his car's repair bills. This was the last chance he had to shoot his fashion and nature photographs. I agreed to help Cigar find a model and shoot some fashion shots myself. Rosa was the tallest girl willing to go with Cigar and me. She was Puerto Rican and from New York and had a crush on Cigar. Cigar told me before we left he thought she was a bit dark, but I assured him she'd be fine; she was bringing a friend who would do the makeup and hair. She didn't like the other white girls in our school, especially the way they pronounced her name. Roze-ahh. She'd say, "Noh! Eeit's RRROS Sa!"

We were supposed to meet Rosa and her friend at school before we left early Saturday morning, the sky still very dark. I hadn't asked who her friend would be, and I thought it would be a girl. Instead, it turned out to be someone that everyone at school ridiculed. His name was John. John was fair-skinned and dyed his hair a yellowish blond. Everyone called him a fag and he didn't seem to fight it. Sometimes the guys would call me a fag, but I'd tell them to fuck off; at worst I'd get in a fight. I just didn't take it like John did. Once in Adult Single Living class, John sat in a circle with the rest of us on the floor. The teacher stopped in the middle of her lecture and asked John to reposition himself. I had no idea what she meant. I looked over at John, who was wearing cut-off, short-short Levi's. John looked down at his crotch and exclaimed, "Oh, she fell out." At which point all the guys near him started to groan and move quickly away from him. John tugged at his shorts, pulling them down his leg, making sure his genitals weren't showing.

Cigar stopped the car away from where Rosa and John were standing, said, "I ain't taking that fag."

I told him it was too late to make different plans. "You need this photo to pass."

Cigar pounded his steering. "No one better fucking say a word to me." The drive across the desert was strangely quiet, consisting of me changing the radio station, and John asking if I'd leave it on KUTE 102, the disco station. I didn't find John so scary, or repulsive. I knew I didn't like him, wouldn't let him have sex with me or anything like that. We walked into a liquor store together. He seemed to be in charge, his eyes held above everyone else's stares, his chin confidently jutted. I noticed as he swiped packages of cookies and chocolate bars into his pockets. I stood at the counter, afraid we'd both get popped for shoplifting, when the cashier asked if that was all I was getting, a bottle of Orange Crush and Necco wafers.

I said yes, but John stopped me, said, "Dear, you forgot the beer." As John walked to the refrigerator doors with beer inside, his walk reminded me of a runway model, the poise with which they carry themselves down the ramp. He returned with two six-packs of Michelob. I raised my eyebrow, sure I was going to get carded. Instead, John tossed onto the counter a MasterCard and said, "Here." The cashier looked at us both, smiled as if embarrassed, and rang us up.

36

As Cigar and Rosa began their shoot, the light just right before the sun went down, John and I lay back onto a dune to rest. John said, "So much for the law-abiding image of the Boy Scouts!" He handed me a cold beer.

I corrected him. "The Explorer Scouts, thank you." I could see Rosa in a pose and I said wait, placing my beer into the sand. From my pocket I pulled out a folded knife. I released the blade, told Rosa to pretend to cut open the top button of her dress. I grabbed my camera and shot a few. Cigar seemed frustrated with my intrusion, so I stopped and went back to my beer.

John said, "You got a good eye."

"Thanks," is all I said.

He acted like he wanted to convince me. "No, really, you could go far."

"Maybe."

John reached over with a finger and grazed my arm. I didn't react. He said, "You're not like the others. Maybe it's because you're artistic." His finger circled my elbow. I took a swig of beer and then belched. This made him stop.

Later that evening we joined the others around camp and set up two tents, one for Cigar and me, the other for Rosa and John. Cigar hung out with the other Explorers while I stayed with Rosa and John. Rosa started in that John should sleep with us since he's a boy and she's a girl. I looked at Rosa and said, "Really, he belongs with you."

John laughed and said, "Let's go walk out to the dune and smoke some pot." We each took a flashlight, our beams crossed over shrubs and sand. I could see Cigar standing around the fire with the others. They stared back at us and started to howl.

John brought a blanket, and he spread it on the slope of the bank, away from camp. From this angle, we could see nothing but darkness and stars. I lay in the middle between Rosa and John. Rosa grabbed my hand and placed it between her knees. She said she was cold, which I could feel from her palms. John lit up a small wooden pipe; the flash from the cigarette lighter illuminated his face for a moment, as did the small glowing bowl of cindery weed. He then placed the pipe at my lips. At first, I reached to hold the pipe myself, but John insisted that he hold the pipe and lighter. The smoke was strong, and for a second I could taste John's finger against my lips as he held the pipe for me for a second hit. John then leaned completely over my body to let Rosa inhale. John's chest was heavy over my own. I could feel his breathing. I could feel how he braced his body with mine. I moved upward, turned to Rosa and kissed her. She returned my kiss with a gentle bite at my lower lip. I held her hand. As I looked at the stars, everything seemed to spin, a falling star shot nearby, and I moved my head as if to duck.

John was at the foot of the dune turning around in circles, his arms twirled like a ballerina. I noticed Cigar and waved to him, but my muscles seemed so heavy and it was so nice to lie next to Rosa. Cigar seemed to be dancing with John and I smiled.

I thought back to the shoot when we came across this old, abandoned shack with a paint-peeled chair. It was my idea to have her wear a bikini and red high heels. It was a gift, I told Cigar, the opening page of his portfolio. I knew the film would expose the wood as blue and if I could get the right lighting on her body, her dark skin would pop. Cigar seemed stunned the way John and I worked together, the way John could visualize what I wanted and put it together on Rosa's face, on Rosa's hair. The way Rosa never seemed offended by the poses I asked her to do, while Cigar's requests were only met halfway or not at all.

I could feel Rosa's cold hand slipping from mine, her saying my name, then John's loudly as if scared. I looked up from the blanket: John and Cigar dancing and I couldn't believe it, Cigar touched John's face again and again.

I'd told Cigar I was giving him this idea because he inspired it— Rosa on the blue chair in a red bikini bottom, arm hooked over the headrest, chair tilted back. With my own hand, I placed Rosa's hand inside her inner thigh and told her I'd be back in a second. Outside, I pulled from my camera bag a stubby cigar. I lit the cigar and hacked strongly. Smoke escaped into the air.

Gently I placed the stubby between Rosa's lips. At first, she wanted to protest, but I hushed her, assured her it would only be a second. Her red lips held the rounded end, the weight of the cigar. John pulled back as if scared, while Cigar moved into position. It was like I had to show Cigar everything, I told him, moving him from shooting up directly between her legs. With firm hands I guided his camera to the side view of her body, later placing my open palms on Cigar's shoulders, at his neck.

John said simperingly, "Hot."

Cigar responded, "Shut up, fag!"

From the desert's darkness, I could see Rosa bringing John up to our blanket, her arm over his shoulders. I could tell she was crying. John's face was held down, his posture no longer like a runway model. He moved his face to where I could see. Blood was running from his nose, the corner of his lips; he was crying also. Cigar was yelling in the desert somewhere, "Fucking faggot, fucking queer!" The sight of John's blood and all the beer we'd had made me nauseous, and I vomited into a bush. From my flashlight, I could see small eyes, darting from bush to bush. I passed my flashlight in that direction and saw they were coyote, gray-coated, sharp teeth, prancing, seething.

They moved close to each other, their mouths touching, gums exposed, as if whispering, telling secrets and rumors. They began to bark, to howl as if in pain.

IF SHE COULD

She would cut out
what is wrong with me;
my body is paper.

She'd leave the edge sharp,
a hollow space at my crotch,
my mouth clean of sperm.

And even her bruiser, my father,
is rock silent about how ill I've become,
claims the plague will clean the cancer.

I tell them about my tumor
scare them with the word "biopsy"
above the lungs, malignant.

"The CAT scans really aren't clear,
and it might be something from birth,
a congenital disorder."

My mother refuses her part,
as if I grew out of a man's weak leg,
nursed on clammy balls and ass.

We weren't put down here for that,
she insists, and if that's prejudice
then it is.

I tell her it's good that we argue,
scissors and paper, mother and son;
but she has to win with the last words.
She says, "It's like you killed me."

A NETLESS HEAVEN

1.

Has it been years already? Bus ride downtown,
head against the rattled window,
and all the passengers whispering
how sad it was, as if to cross themselves;
fortune read in blood.
I was sick, tie loose around my neck,
yellow phlegm coughed into tissue,
pillbox time alarm.
The bus driver leaned back, strained to hear
the young woman, business skirt
small radio in hand, "Magic has HIV."
When I got home, Mother had already called;
redlight answer machine flashed,
cries in the message, her favorite player
his smile, never will be the same.
Underneath covers, my bones hurt;
cradled the phone, she said,
he'll do a lot of good, he'll beat this thing—
and like an unspooled movie I saw she didn't cry
when I told her, face furrowed in disappointment,
said she knew I'd end like this.

2.

Sunday school catechism,
the Father would have us play

for an hour, to wind us down
to hard wooden seats, chalkboard
words, the act of contrition,
rosary beads on name-carved desks.
He kneeled behind me on the asphalt,
his black cloth chest humped my back,
guided my blundering hands around the basketball;
the flesh of his palms burned.
I could feel his holy water breath
soft as feather wings brushed along
the jugular of my neck.
When I released the ball to a netless heaven
he didn't respond, just pulled the next boy
close to him, graced his hand under the boy's chin.

PARROTS

Walking to my therapist,
his San Marino office, the streets lined
with bougainvillea, apricots,
steam clouds from the steam plant.
Here the power lines haven't been buried
and the parrots spend their summer
on the electrical wires, squawking and shitting.
No one can sleep in on any day, we're all red-eyed,
the birds caw wild, mark territory, sounds
of a South American war, no natural enemy.
I'm cautious as I pass under feathered rears.
A shirtless man hangs from his window,
hands pressed together, pointed up.
Gun metal pulls at the sun,
a hostage to reflection.
He aims at the flashes of green,
yellow, red, fires.

My therapist says it's okay to hate your parents
their nightly battles, the bedroom stuffy
and always my father slept with me in the end.
Even now I parrot their fighting in my lovers' quarrels,
find pieces of their seed hanging off me
claws, beaks, feathers, crap.
It doesn't take a genius to make sense of the gun.

III

The jungle is lush and it cries.

HIS ONLY FAMILY

We smoke Raleighs along the cement bank
river, near the young bamboo growth; here
the sun is bright, bouncing off my mirrored
glasses, the water's surface, and John's
watch. She is new to this game of telling
the truth; she was raising kids on Lake Elsinore,
letting hair sprout under her arms, teaching
the girls about baseball like a father would.
She was John's closest sister; they'd slept
together at ages one and two, skated on
Michigan's lakes, traded nasty words like
greeting cards, learned to smoke the French
way, all so sophisticated and glamorous.
California does that to you, I say, makes your skin
pliable, lazy and sun-drenched. It's the
shade that you need every now and then;
John leans over and kisses me fully on the
mouth, his tongue darting in, and I take it.
Mary looks away in disgust, throws her cigarette
into the water as if to start a gasoline fire.
She says, why are you doing this to me; it'll
break Mom and Dad's hearts.

We make a retreat to the parents' trailer
home; kids are running through screen doors,

brothers are watching football passes. Everyone
just stares at me and I can't find a place to sit
so I knock over some books and a statue of
Eisenhower. The coffee maker is filled again;
it pisses in the air. I'm already jittery with
caffeine. I corner myself in the kitchen
and listen to the women talking about cousin
Kate's affair, aunt Marge's hysterectomy, how
the next wedding will come off. John pulls me,
rushes me to the back room, lined with
canning jars, lids and seals, a shelf full of
cling peaches. He tells me I'm the only one
in his life, his only family; I start to cry.
He leaves me alone; the late noon wind cuts through
the broken windows, the pierced gray screens,
the spaces between the jars, filling my lungs
with syrupy air and the air is all I need for
that moment; it lets explosions happen,
fires burn.

BUZZ

The steamed milk froth spills over the cup's lip.
My table shakes, even with a napkin
folded twice under the leg. A man's eyes
are green next to the window and he smiles,
reading the Sunday *Times*, sips his cappuccino;
foam gathers on his mustache, peppered white.

I tear a package of sugar, granulated and white,
pour in a spiral, can see he's wiping his lips.
People clamor, carrying journals and cappuccinos.
Spilled liquid at my table soaks a stack of napkins.
I lift my writing tablet. He flips his page, smiles.
The sun is strongest on his face, catches in the eyes.

The music, loud, Latin jazz, contact made by our eyes.
I turn shy, my hands dark around the ceramic's white.
As if this was all he needed, he folds his paper, smiles,
getting ready to leave, instead brings the cup to his lips.
I debate, think of how to leave my number on a napkin,
a kiss staining the corner, the color of cappuccino.

I roll over a fresh sheet, pen tapping my cappuccino.
People laugh as they bump my table, I draw eyes,
nose and mouth, blue ink rips into a napkin.
I should be working on the page, it curls bare and white.

The lines tease me, and I begin to think of his lips.
I notice him at the counter, he looks my way and smiles.

I write how I see him, the look of his hands, his smile.
Over the music, the sound of steamed milk for cappuccinos.
I weave a story where he puts a madeleine to my lips,
how the sunlight creates windows in his green eyes.
My dark hands show how his fingers are so white.
The milky froth dapples his mustache, I give him my napkin.

I look at what I've written, instead draw on my napkin.
It's all too sad, this writer's block, so I smile.
I imagine an outcome, where our drinks stain the whites
of our shirts and we order more cappuccinos,
shaky from all the caffeine, nervousness shows in our eyes.
I steady myself, send cool breaths over the cup's lip.

He comes to my table. I press my lips to a napkin.
Our eyes swirl, coffee and cream, and he smiles,
sips his cappuccino on a saucer of white.

NECTARINES AND ORCHIDS

for Kevin

We melt like savages together
legs folding, teeth bared
and he is grunting in my face.
I bite into his shoulder,
his neck, his ears
and he slips in another finger
as if that is what I had wanted,
knuckle by knuckle, till I am open
and unpretentious.
It makes the hasty bedsheets,
the Brazil 67, the whole room
smell of summer and sweat,
too hot to touch.
The cats just walk on by,
their tails loping in the humid air,
so I scratch deep and hard,
his back arched,
his mouth a hole
where my tongue passes lips
and I taste fruit,
a crush of petals and meat.
The jungle is lush and it cries.

FEBRUARY 15, 1992

The rain knocked out my telephone
and I didn't notice all day. Kept the TV on
while Jeffrey Dahmer's verdict
was broadcast, side stories of skinning dogs,
a chocolate factory, early photos
with his shirt taken off. He was sane,
the unseen jury decided, and the victim's families,
all Black, held each other's hands in chain,
each wondering what part had been taken out,
their gay sons in the stomach of evil.

My stomach hurt all day,
twisted as if green inside, my shit
the color of wheat. I jerked off
to see if that would help me feel better.

It was late when my lover came home,
debated if we wanted to see a performance
at the Episcopal church, the show's title
made of animals, a minotaur, an alien.
It was some multicultural event, the troupe,
Latinos and Blacks, in all-white Pasadena.
But ten dollars seemed extravagant
to be told of AIDS, racism, homophobia,
and other ills, masks like folk art
the audience wonders where they could buy.

IT'S FRIDAY NIGHT AND JESUS IS AT THE LAUNDROMAT

I'm separating loads
between darks and lights
when she tells me God's inside her
breeding salvation.
Her legs hang over my washer's edge
and I shove in as many quarters
as it takes to get her going,
fleshy kneecaps rotate,
magazine pages vibrate.
Her calling card says, *Joeseph,*
you'll never get a better proposition,
and like dogma
she parts her thighs
giving me a good glimpse,
telling me no man
has ever touched her before.

MICKEY AND PLUTO UNDRESS BEHIND THE WALLS OF SLEEPING BEAUTY CASTLE

Mickey's face is the first to come off.
He is sweaty around his neck;
his large, white gloves are tossed to the tile floor.
Slowly he starts to unbutton the rest of his furry body.

Pluto, dog-tired, discards his hindquarters,
revealing the legs and calves of a real man.
He hooks his tail up in a locker, alongside the others,
row after row of fantasy creatures,
skins without volume, retired from the pawing,

the petting, cannon flashes and constant waving.
All he wants to do now is slip out of his briefs,
grab a wink and go to the bars.
He begins to remove his collar, but that's when
Mickey, now fully human, unleashes the leather strap,

letting the ears and wet nose fall.
The next day, they return to Main Street,
their deep red mouths are open and friendly,
kissing the silky tops of children's heads,
smiling for cameras that begin to rewind.

SUCKING

On his skin, his shoulder
blood peeks through pores,
my tongue smears, salivates,
then removes: all I can manage
is "Oh," my mouth a gash,
his flesh broken.
he's infected
and so am I, I
have my own viral strain
encoded in cell
and bone
hard for him.
Will not believe what has happened,
rinse in the sink several times,
look for the water to be stained
red, running in pipe
organ, ocean
marrow. I return to bed
convince myself
there weren't any open sores,
my gums tight
I didn't swallow.
He changes into clothes
a love bite, hidden
under a short-sleeve cuff,

then he's gone
before I turn to something worse
the result of build-up, reinfection
damage done by hunger, risk
I can't control
my need for him
pull back
and starve.

IV

It makes me cry at God, stain the earth.

CHEAP RENT

One of the tenants, a single woman
vacuums the hallways for a break in rent
while another maintains the laundry room.
We constantly meet on the stairs;
she huffs, and I pause for my heart.
Still another tenant, who shall remain
nameless, takes care of the garden
behind the apartment, a small patio
of flower boxes, decorative stones,
a weather-worn bench.

My bedroom window overlooks the garden
and I've watched this thin, swarthy man
dig out all his plants, arrange them
in some random new order: where
once stood a poinsettia, there's now a plumbago,
then a monstera, then a hydrangea.
The only thing predictable is the rosemary,
thrusting out of the soil like small interruptions
between the more tended, transitory foliage.
Sometimes I borrow a few sprigs, use in soups,
sprinkle the dry leaves into sauces, rub them
against the flesh of chicken. At night
I place them in my bath. The man told me
it's good for all evils in the body. He cuts sprays

of small blue flowers, his hands tense on shears.
I lay my glasses on the tub's edge,
stems graze my thighs. He tells me
it's especially good for the heart.

DETACHED

for Bill, whom I met at an AIDS support group

This time of year, night fell at seven;
We'd lie on the floor, beneath the church
on cushions we stole from the music room.
As a class of twenty men, we believed
the mind could heal, that infections
could be held back, that there were powers
and if we had conviction, we had hope.
In the dark, we saw our cells, fuchsia, cerise,
growing like flowers in spring,
burgeoning, our blood invincible, renewed.
After the session, Bill and I would eat the town—
Barney's Beanery, Ernie's Taco House, the Japanese Ai.
We were both ARC, one step away
from full-blown lesions, pneumonia, and death,
one step beyond HIV safety and "just only positive."
As if it were a sin we ordered sushi,
aware of its dangers, and I had a beer
that made me dizzy and moist, my palms wet.
He stared across the table.
I wanted to hold both of his hands and laugh.
We talked about computers, software,
our lovers. His lover died in December too,
just like John, and Bill was as old as John
and I was as old as Pablo; we were both doing well,
learning about our bodies, our disease, our chances

of survival, watching our classmates drop,
too sick to continue, too disinterested to be led.
Later on, Bill caught a flu he couldn't shake;
I was scared to see the muscles in his face fall
into socket and bone, his arms, stick and veins,
the fevers and chills, the long gaps of time
where I wouldn't see him, and I was always surprised
at the amount of weight he had lost, like water.
One day he said it was CMV
that it gets into the lungs and marrow,
the liver and brain; he said he was weak,
that he had pains in his stomach,
that it was opportunistic, that he now had AIDS.
After that, I couldn't concentrate on the bridge
in my mind, the one that led to freedom
and health, or so claimed the audiotapes
of smooth music and coma words, that said
that you allow yourself to be sick,
that it is rooted in your hate, that you hate yourself.

DIS(COLORATION)

WHEN MY DOCTOR told me "MAI," I was shocked. I never thought I'd get that. My very good friend had died recently of it, and we had both tested at about the same time. I've handled other diagnoses much better, being responsible, seeing what the side effects were of any new drug, how others felt about the medication. Not this time. After a few months of Lamprene, I noticed that even during the coldest part of the year, I came off as having a fabulous tan. At first it was golden, then a burnt sienna. It looked exotic; people thought I had sold a life insurance policy and gone to Bermuda.

My folks, on the other hand, were a little displeased. I grew up in Montebello; my parents raised me to be as American as possible, not teaching us Spanish, encouraging us to always say we are American. Most of my extended family still lived in the rural section of the state with other descendants of migrant workers. One summer my cousins came down to L.A. to visit us. My aunt and mother clucked about how much darker her boys were compared to me; they called them "Negroes."

I figured that was a bad thing to be, but my cousins were so much fun; they pulled me into their games outside, the "Slide and Splash," till I started to burn. My mother dragged me back inside. "You don't want to look like those boys, do you? I'd be so embarrassed."

Now grown up, I'm not light-skinned anyway. And with Lamprene, I always get questioned about where I'm from. In the beginning, it was enjoyable. I'd tell people my father was Chicano and my mother was Berber, or half Hindu and Polynesian. I would get oohs and ahhs from my audience. Their belief would prod me on to say, "All the men in my family have this look."

With AIDS, you have to watch for anything unsightly. And in this "Age Defying" culture, as Revlon would have it, I am not without my vanity. Any new product that suggests youth-restoring properties I will run out and purchase. I have tubes and creams and soaps that rival the amount of my medicines, and the bathroom is not large enough for both. I can go on for hours about the different alpha hydroxy tubes, creams, capsules, masks that are available and I have. I say all this to bring up the point: I know what my face looks like, up close, in the mirror.

I noticed that my Lamprene wasn't giving me the glow I was used to; people now came up to me and asked me what's that on my forehead. I remember the first morning it became apparent, I screamed. I looked like an old man who had dyed his hair black, and the dye dribbled down the forehead and sideburns. It was truly hideous. I looked like a guest alien on *Star Trek*. I searched for any cosmetic in my collection that could help, but nothing did. In the daytime, I took to wearing baseball caps pulled all the way to my eyebrows, *très chic*? While walking to my doctor's office in Century City, I passed a drugstore with a huge display of cosmetics. I thought I'd take a chance and see if they had any fading cream. I remembered watching *Soul Train* and one of the products they promoted was a cream that fades dark patches on Black women's faces. That seemed like the thing for me. But alas, no cream at this store. The saleswoman said, "Why don't you try a store in a more predominantly Black neighborhood?"

My part of town isn't predominantly Black, but there are African Americans, not like in Montebello. I walked swiftly through the pharmacy to the aisle where all the skin care products were. No luck. By chance, while looking for a good gel for my hair, I noticed it, between the pomade and curl relaxer—Ambi Fade Cream. I was surprised by its economical cost; I haven't spent that little on a beauty product in years. I picked the tube that looked the most pleasing. It showed a side view of a young African American woman with smooth, even-toned skin. The others had weird doctor names and came in unattractive packaging. I figured they were inferior. Having rung it up, the cashier hardly gave me another look. I had in mind to tell her it was for my girlfriend, but I'd have had to lower my voice.

Taking the tube home quickly, I read the instruction and put a small dab on my finger. I rubbed it on my forehead. The cream didn't seem to absorb in my skin and left a white film that sort of made the effect seem pale. After weeks of using the ointment—the instructions said it may take many applications—I noticed round patches of clear spots. "NOW," I complained, "I look like I have polka dots!"

I'm sort of getting used to the look, forgetting to put on the cream some nights. The skin area has dried up and left flaky patches I've scratched off. When I'm in the mood, I tell people that my father is Chicano and my mother, well my mother is from another planet, and all the men in her family have this unusual skin design.

DOPPELGÄNGER

THE EARLIEST MEMORY of the intruder occurred the last time I was in the hospital. I had been breathing irregularly for the last few weeks, hyperventilating, hacking up yellowish phlegm. When I had a checkup with my doctor, he found nothing and thought my lungs sounded fine and strong.

Marcus was concerned as I went through bottles of grape-flavored cough syrup, bags of lemon drops, and gallons of bitter ginger tea; he insisted one night that I go to the emergency room at the nearby hospital. By that time it was apparent; blood pressure was off. I could barely string more than three words together before I had to gasp for breath. I was immediately put into a thinly covered hospital bed, TV remote on my right, bed control on the left. My nostrils were tubed and fine streams of moist oxygen were pumped from the wall behind the bed covered with other medical gadgetry, overhead lamps, blood pressure sleeve and gauge, various plugs for lifeline machines, IVs. For the moment it felt good to lie within the cool sheets of the hospital bed, my feet raised slightly, my back angled gently up. The New Zealander nurse who attended my needs brought me delicious chicken sandwiches, glasses of crushed ice with water and lemon slices. She let me watch my favorite TV program before she painlessly extracted the twelve vials of blood into various-sized tubes with colored tops, all needed to start the many tests I was to undergo.

That night I dreamt my mother was yelling down at my youngest brother, the one I feel closest to, almost fatherly. As the red-infused dream of my mother's tirade went on, her face changed into a bloody distortion, the creases in her face and forehead looked as if carved with a hatchet. She held a knife, a long, familiar kitchen knife that was the sharpest blade she had when we were children and she could cut whole chicken parts with it, breaking the joints, slicing easily through the flesh. Once she cut herself badly with this knife. She did not scream or cry; she simply clenched her finger under the faucet and the blood swirled in the sink with the juice of the pulled-out chicken neck and brown giblets.

As if mirrored silk, the knife slid through my brother's rib cage, revealing organs still throbbing, like holy cards of Catholic martyrs. My voice became enclosed in old black lead. I wanted to scream the harshest words I could use; my face dripped jewel-like tears while my body thrashed. Still, mother kept on stabbing and slashing, the knife slicing through bone, severing arteries and creating spigots of shooting blood. My heart ceased as if being crushed between two firm hands. I was afraid to approach them, my brother's skin draped across her feet. And like a magnet I was drawn to her. I hunched down to protect my own chest, deforming myself, as I have done my whole life, when she would strike me across the mouth for sayings smart things, making sure I knew who ruled my life, enforcing that I had to be perfect in everyone else's eyes except hers because she knew how worthless and pathetic I was.

My New Zealander nurse touched my arm gently. "Do you always have night sweats so badly?" The sheet that had been covering me was sopping wet and smelled strangely of my body, tin cans, and cayenne pepper. Now being changed, the memory of the dream had left real tears as evidence. I wiped my face dry with a corner of the sheets.

Twelve more empty vials were placed next to me; with tender movements she began to tie off my arm with a stretched latex glove. Muscles of my upper arm winced, circulation stopped, and my hand became numb. I turned away to the window, the mini-blind slats still open; night having fallen hours earlier, Hollywood's klieg lights circled the skies above like vultures.

The doctor stood in the room, clipboard tilted so only he could see the results of tests. He was stocky, with black curly hair and a large bulbous nose. He tapped his nose with a single finger and then spoke. He was very concerned about why I was on such heavy antidepressants and another psych-oriented drug. I told him of my lifelong history of depression, my earliest experience at six years old, how I would lock myself in dark rooms, speak to no one. The doctor listened carefully, then inquired, "And the voices?"

I had to beg his pardon, because I didn't understand what he was asking. "The other drug you are taking is for people who hear voices in their head."

I sat there stunned. I told him, I had been informed that this particular drug was considered a mood elevator. He shook his head and pursed his lips. "No, and if you've been on this drug for as long as you claim, I'm surprised you don't have any serious mouth movement disorders. That's the long-term side effect, your mouth develops twitches."

I told him, "I remember telling my doctor I heard voices when I had cryptococcal meningitis, which is obviously affecting the brain, but I haven't heard voices since after treatment." Turning toward the door, he suggested that when I got out of the hospital I should see a psychiatrist and work myself off this drug; the antidepressant was my choice, however.

Some of the best drug experiences I've ever had were in the hospital. When I was suffering from shingles, I screamed for Demerol shots. It was lovely. With meningitis, the same drug of choice. But with pneumonia, they decided Halcyon was best for me. I was told it would help regulate my breathing better; my constant hiccups would end. It would relax me.

I stared across to Marcus, who was making a valiant effort to be there for me as much as he could; even though our area was having the worst winter in recent times, he'd come. The rains drenched his clothes, staining his shoulders, the calves of his legs. The buses he had to take were always late and crowded and he complained of people coughing without covering their mouths. He would bring me movies, snacks, my CD player, magazines that had only pictures.

Still, something deeper was troubling him, but with the Halcyon, I could not fathom it. My room turned into a Salvador Dalí painting; clocks melted like processed sliced cheese. Small silver discs would appear at the edge of my vision, and when I turned, they would dart the other way. All of a sudden two statues would appear in my room; sometimes they would be classical Greek gods, other times, hideous unfamiliar entities. My ex-lover would call and then he'd be there in front of me immediately, then gone again. I began to sleep like children sleep, or maybe I was the newly dead.

RECOVERY

I.
Kevin steadies me while I make my way.
The hospital room dark,
unfamiliar furniture,
small windows, clouds.
I roll with my IV attached;
the stand scratches the bed's metal paws,
sparks fly, infusions slosh,
the plastic bags above.
Our feet are wrapped,
tangled in tubes, simple feeds
lead to a vein.
My arm is inflamed from the pull.
The bathroom light switch glows;
it warns of possibilities
of what's wrong with me,
shadows in X-rays,
corners of eyes turned black,
my blood is a threat to me.
But his arm is gentle, cool
around my waist, his hands
slip my underwear off.
At once I shit,
piss, vomit;
long streams of yellow mucus

flow out of nostril
and land on my feet,
the brown tile,
Kevin's open palms.
Tears break from his eyes;
my heart is decimated.
I am spent.

2.
I wait for more tests,
ten vials of blood
skin allergy injection, razor cuts
timed, then a simple operation,
invasive, anesthetized.
I am unwashed, filthy
and as much as Kevin strokes
the white cloth over my legs
and arms pricked with needle wounds,
gunk from bandages and tape,
my face will still stay sickly.
My fingers touch grease.
In the corner of my eyes
yellow scum, little black worms
float over retinas. I pretend to be blind,
shut tight, colors ignite, patterns emerge.
I can hear other men in this ward
struggle for air, taste their medication
in the atmosphere, my tongue metallic.
TVs on for hours,
there is no calm or quiet here.
Wheels and footsteps,
orderlies wait at my door.
I chuckle at how gentle they are with me,

"Careful," they say.
I open my eyes, notice
as my clothes,
an Angelica robe, are removed,
that bones define my body now,
papier-mâché man
from Day of the Dead.
I can hardly move my arms to help,
to lift myself from the bed,
Kevin's strength is there for me;
I imagine he could cradle me in his arms.
I am that light.

3.
I ask Kevin to follow me
down to surgery,
to hold my hand through corridors and elevator.
I can only see light bars pass above
like seconds
marked, precious for their own sake.
He holds back and I twist for him,
head turned sharp.
He is red-faced,
his eyes have grown old and fearful.
"I'll be all right, honey," I plead.
The last door forbids his entrance now,
our separation rushed,
sliced apart as if nothing;
the touch of his hand lingers over my mouth.

Inside, the color of the walls changes;
I shiver under three rough blankets.
Lights are arranged above me.

The doctor speaks of minor risk;
he wants to cut out a piece of my lung,
no bigger than a dot,
or a period I might make.
I will bleed, he tells me,
cough up saliva and phlegm;
my lungs could collapse,
mortality is one in seven thousand.
Fumes curl in the plastic mask, my savior.
It prevents me from thinking, even dreaming.
What feels like a second goes by;
I can hear my name being called. "Gilbert, wake up."
It's not Kevin's voice, but the nurse's.
On the wall's valance,
the word "Recovery" is posted, font bold and large.
When I awoke, I knew I'd bleed, my voice
scraped to almost grunts, a whisper.
I knew Kevin would not be there,
that lovers need to earn money to live
and our silver wedding bands are seen just as parody.
It's as if the doctor removed some vital tissue,
a lining that could never heal
or a leaf that falls from stem.

PALEONTOLOGY

for Michael Niemoeller

We are like two brothers in a riverless canyon
searching for fossils, old whale skeletons,
worn-through work gloves, impressions of lost cities.
My bare knees cut against the dry rocks,
leave skin and blood wherever I go.
You wear creased khakis, neat and dust-free—
Mother's favorite boy. With small pick
and painter's brush you expose objects of beauty
so easily; unbroken vessels
appear in your palms, glint under the sun.
I feel I am slow, clumsy,
struggling to stay attached to the wall;
worthless stones fall between my fingers.
You work diligently. I watch how you breathe,
feel exhaustion in your swollen muscles,
see the silver crucifix move tightly
around your throat. Part of me
resents how simply you free these artifacts.
Still, I break dirt clods in my hands, find
A small tooth, hooked like a shark's,
and a fierce beast grows from there,
jagged tail lashes out, angry and articulate.
You always approved, came over
from your work to admire mine.
Jealousy made me believe it was only to rest,

your flesh unable to sweat, to excrete
the body's toxins. I would have marked you
if I'd grabbed onto your limbs,
meat dimpling over yellow bones.
But now I see you in this rock face,
no longer at my side. I uncover the birdcage
architecture of your chest. Your hand
of umbrella wires clutches an oak stylus
that cannot rest; clay tablets
of written language disintegrate. I brush you out
with careful breath and the edge of my small finger
because it hurts to see wrists form from stone,
the radius and ulna of your arms. And then
there is your face, empty sockets,
skin curling away from jaw,
your smile.
It makes me cry at God,
stain the earth like a storm
from the north, cold tears
you would have heard first
hit the ground.

NEED

I.

THE LARGE-FACED CLOCK drips down the sunlit teal wall. The round timepiece oozes into an oval; its arms bend downward as if drugged. A brilliantly white male nurse in tight white jeans walks into my room, adjusts the tubing of my IV stand so it will stop crying. As he bends over, I stare at the top of his silky blond hair, the white collar of his polo shirt hugging the muscles of his neck. His back looks wide and powerful, a disguise, I imagine, to hide what were once angel wings, cut off so he could walk this earth. In a small white paper cup, he offers another white pill, another few hours of reverie to stop the intense muscle spasms. Half my body is covered with blankets, while my left leg, chest, and arm are bare. The nurse touches my legs with a small stroke, outlining the tattoo on my calf, saying it is beautiful. I tell him it is a Roman design meant to ward off evil spirits, illness. The double trident design is blood red, with tips colored in blue. I can see the pink of his fingernails moving along the intricate pattern, moving slowly up my leg. I look into his eyes and notice I can't make out their color, the room's large windows reflecting white squares in his pupils. He presses his cool palm on the upper part of my thigh and leaves it there while his other hand brushes hair from my forehead. He then lets his fingers glide over the indentations of my cheekbones. My breathing is slow, no longer the strained endeavor it had been when I was checked in. I begin to think I could fall in love with this man, someone who wouldn't be afraid when I became ill, would hold me in his lap while I died. His lips part as his face moves closer to mine and I look up as if he is going to say something truly important. I strain to hear the sounds of bells and flutes, water crashing and the hum only heard while in deep meditation, the body having fallen away, useless. I shoot up into the atmosphere, my eyesight blind as if staring into a flashbulb. I dream in an empty void.

2.

I first met Craig the night of Christmas Eve. The sun had just gone down, and the coolness of winter was beginning to bite. He stood outside where all the other people with HIV gathered for the party that night, an outing at the Green Hotel to celebrate Christmas. He stood with a man I hardly knew; he seemed imposing, strong-willed as I came up to say hello to David or Daniel, I couldn't remember his name. It was funny; later I realized that D had mentioned he had a crush on this man. But it had gone nowhere; what D said he liked most of all about Craig was his brutal honesty. I figured out later this was like a wish to be abused by Craig, to hear all the worst qualities of himself expressed by Craig. D turned away from me after he said hello. Craig moved forward, said he liked my smile. He stood in a beautiful gray suit with pinstripes. He seemed a foot taller than me, enough to make me feel a twinge of intimidation, but Craig's own smile only made me smile more, his large mustache giving him a daddy look. His voice was like gunfire celebrating some rebel victory, deep and manly. We stood the whole night in the lush hotel lobby talking about everything from gardens to architecture. Of our past loves and how they all died.

3.

Craig is there when I wake; he's unshaven. The TV is on, and I can barely hear the whisper of the actors' dialogue. It is a movie I've been trying to watch but I've only seen sections and not in order. Here a man who seems like the devil is making pacts with unsuspecting souls

77

along this highway, recording his conquests through Polaroids; the victims' faces all look anguished. Craig reaches into his backpack and pulls out a large beer bottle. Our eyes lock for a moment and he says with strained humor, "Well, she's finally up." He looks downward and shrugs his shoulders as he pours beer into a paper cup. I notice his hands, so strong normally; they now look bony and frail. I reach for the bed's control, adjusting the position so that I can sit up. I ask him what day it is. He says slowly, "Thursday." I count to myself how long I've been in, a week and a half, maybe a day more. I close my eyes and Craig sighs, "Maybe I should just come back later."

I tell him, "No, no, no."

He then says, "I've been here for hours already, and you don't need me."

"Just talk to me," I plead.

He takes a sip of his beer. "I called last night, do you remember?" I shake my head no. "You kept on calling me John, saying how you needed me, and then you'd say John. It's like he's not dead to you and I'm some kind of replacement. I can't believe you when you say you love me. I don't feel it." The creases around Craig's eyes tighten, and he looks down into his beer.

I tell him it's not fair, I was drugged out, the Thorazine makes me hallucinate.

Craig pauses. "Maybe it is truly how you feel. I can't blame you for that. It's like he's always there in my face. I can't be him. I'm struggling too with this disease, my neuropathy is always hurting, I'm always broke. I can't give you shit. I can't even make it easier for you; your doctors won't tell me anything. They keep on expecting to see John taking care of you and who am I? John gave you everything; what can I do in comparison?"

I look at my arm, where the IV curves like a snake to the top of my wrist. I can feel the pinprick, hear the IV pump churning in chemicals, and I'm so embarrassed. Tears are running down my face. I can feel shit coming out my ass. I try to move but I am so weak I can't move quickly enough. I blurt out, "Can you help me?"

Craig moves close to me, "What's going on?"

"I need to go to the bathroom." He lifts me by the shoulder, bearing most of my weight. I start chanting, "I just want to die, die." I have no strength; I can feel shit running down my leg. My stomach turns in nausea. "Fuck." As Craig unties my gown I can smell sulfur. My bony ass hits hard the toilet seat and it hurts. I start letting loose my bowels, what control I have left. In panic I reach for a bucket that's under the sink and start puking; urine painfully trickles out from my dick.

Craig keeps on telling me it's OK, holding my hand tight; my stomach churns more. I think back to just a few weeks ago on a Sunday. We had gone to the cemetery to walk around, the weather slightly cloudy and cool. It had been a place he told me he always liked to go by himself, that I was the first person that he could share this with. He loved walking among the graves, smelling the copal incense burning in cups of aluminum foil, straightening the wilting flowers left a while back. He especially loved Marion Davis's crypt, how most people didn't know it was hers because they used her family name, Durvas. At the front of the cemetery, there was a boysenberry tree, shaped like an open umbrella, with long branches hanging to the ground. It was burdened with almost ripe berries, slightly more red than purple. We stood underneath the canopy picking berries, our fingers becoming stained from the juice. Visitors would walk by and stare at what we were doing. At first, I thought that we shouldn't be doing it, that somehow we would get in trouble. Still Craig would lift branches for me to pick; his movements were so sure, confident that it made me feel no one could say we were doing something wrong. The berries were sweet and juicy, the product of the long rainy season of winter and spring, so unusual for this climate, and before Craig could turn away, I kissed him, gently and brief. He seemed embarrassed by my sudden show of emotion, again lifting a branch as if to change the subject, offering me the darkest berry. As sweet juice erupted in my mouth, I remembered a poem[1]:

> They don't think they're too tough or desperate,
> They know that the law always wins;
> They've been shot at before,
> But they do not ignore
> That death is the wages of sin.
>
> Some day they'll go down together;
> And they'll bury them side by side;
> To few it'll be grief—
> To the law a relief—
> But it's death for Bonnie and Clyde.

---

1 Bonnie Parker, "The Story of Suicide: The Ballad of Bonnie and Clyde."

V

Coming closer like footsteps near a locked door.

UNUSUAL JUNE WEATHER IN L.A.

The weathermen nearly came in their pants, their
satellite eyes tripped across the sky.
Spittle slipped from the corners of their mouths every
newscast. Drizzle was on its way.

It was true, clouds were present all day. The small puffs
reminded me of Lucky Charms—horseshoes,
clovers, pots of gold. As currents scudded
the charms, Timothy Leary's face began to form,
a miraculous vision like Jesus risen
or Mary in tree sap's blood.
I had heard Timothy's ashes would be shot into space,
he was halfway there, from stars we come, to stars we return.
A chill ran through me
as he laughed above. Strange,
the man whose final motto was "Dial On, Tune In, Hang Out,
Link Up, Escape-Delete" would be reborn an innocent cloud.
The wind chimes around the block rang, church bells
struck for Mass, till he was gone, dissolved,
nothing special, no drizzle for the land,
and memory simply evaporated under a typical warm sun.

EVEN MY FATHER PUT DOWN HIS
BEER FOR THIS

I remember running around my bedroom
on top of beds, over chairs
looking out the window
trying to find the source
of the low-pitched hum
that shook the house
to its tract-built foundation
and made my mother yell at me,
"What the hell are you doing in that room?"
like I would cause the house to fall.

Then BOOM!
as if a 747 had crashed
gas pipes exploded
streets caught fire,
or the Russians started a rain
of bombs, first on Montebello, East L.A.,
Pico Rivera, then the rest of the world.
There was never enough time to hide,
attack was swift as a slap.
I threw back the curtains
to watch the sky boil,
but all that was out front
was Mrs. Flores's floppy rose bushes
and Mr. Bellows walking Scout
his tiny, mixed dachshund.

My mother looked outside timidly
as did the other neighbors,
peeping out peepholes,
looking north to the freeway.
The women began to fix their hair,
the men tucked in shirts, buckled pants,
even my father put down his beer for this.
My mother showed her different face
the one with softer angles, fuller lips
and we walked to the scene,
three abreast, a family.
Everyone was there, holding noses,
gagging on the duckish air.
We stared at the chemical truck
cracked open, an enormous black egg
with ooze seeping down the sides
pouring over a small Nova,
its wipers blinking like eyes.
On the freeway's bank
scattered in the wheatgrass
were metal shell pieces
and Mr. Richards held a chunk
that landed on his driveway.
He kept saying, "Just look at this mess."
My mother worried that it would explode again,
staining the walkways,
the wood-shingled roofs.
She told my father her stomach was sour.
He said his throat burned.

When the hook and ladder started to hose the lanes,
my mother began to talk with other women
arms crossed under breast,

their eyes on a fireman or two.
My father yammered with the guys
slapping backs
giving a good shake to everyone's grip,
inviting a few home for a drink.
They sat on patio chairs
in front of the garage,
my father's Coleman filled with Bud.
And all us kids got out bikes
rode around the neighborhood
near the explosion, the Fire Chief,
the news reporter from channel 5.
We flew off curbs,
skidded on sidewalks,
ran over lawns.
Even Mrs. Flores didn't mind us on her grass.
She didn't turn on the sprinklers
till after the fire trucks left;
my father passed out,
and Scout barked at the moon.

BOTERO IN BEVERLY HILLS

The men in my family, American born
but still Latin, admire women
round and fleshy. The rear ends,
breasts, and thighs are Thanksgiving,
Easter, and Christmas devoured
with finger-sucked gratification,
their bedsheets a place of fine cuisine.
Still there is something abundantly roguish
about women reclined, mirror in hand,
bronze legs thick as surrounding tree trunks,
statuesque butts wide like the fleet of Mercedes
and BMWs on the fine paved streets of Beverly Hills.
My brothers crane their necks out my car window
as if to whistle catcalls and other obscenities,
realize the unapproachability of these heavyweights,
and sigh as they would passing a fast-food joint.
The only nude male is of a Trojan,
a small protuberance for a penis
shaped like the end of a funnel.
He is like all the rest, corpulent
with small ankles and wrists,
someone easily knocked down, made to cry.
For the rest of the day, I'll keep to my diet,
iced tea, garden salad, dressing on the side.
My lover will grill skinless chicken on

the hibachi perched over the rail of our veranda.
My brothers however will return to their wives,
sabotage the women's caloric intake
bring home hamburgers and apple pies
instead of red roses or the gorgeous little
emerald their wives saw in the club store catalogue
that they'd pleaded for just that morning.

JUSTICE IS A WHITE WOMAN

Blind,
you can feel ash
fall along your spine.
You are able to distinguish
the scent of your child
from any other,
his sweat familiar as your own.
From distances
you hear glass break open,
splash against sidewalks,
dropped like old-fashioned bottles
of babies' milk,
cradled to the heart,
a memory of white.
Tonight, out your window,
gunshot, backfire, pot exploding
on the stove, you are not sure.
There are screams,
but you've learned to ignore them:
the neighbor and her boyfriend,
the son and his mother,
every father's arrival.
Sirens are endless
and everywhere you turn,
smoke.

In the morning
you hear the word "justice"
from all the apartments
in your building.
Random voices caught,
a dog's bark across the street,
phrases in Chinese and Spanish;
arguments rise like heat
from the floors below.
Inside, children play tattered board games,
Risk and Concentration,
parents wrestle through news breaks,
helicopter views, *Live over Downtown.*

You remember being a small girl;
a teacher placed a statue
in your hands, guided your fingers
the length of a sword,
the balance of a scale.
Slowly, he led you over the breast,
down the legs' seams,
to fall upon bare feet.
Tenderly on the face,
he held your touch where cloth
had been tied over the woman's eyes.
Cheap plaster powder
rubbed off in your hands,
his beard grazed your cheek,
the corner of your mouth.
He said, "She is just like you."
The blow of his breath
made you think you touched fire.
Your hands let go,

the small statuette
becoming sound.
Quickly you tried to recover,
remorse in your stomach.
How dim fingers had to seek
along the room's corners,
beg the fragments to fit,
each dull piece laid out,
tried one at a time.
Still more slivers missed
your passing hand,
stay undiscovered.

BLACK HELICOPTERS

I have seen them out the corners of my eyes;
they float near the horizon,
pass freeways, head for the desert.
Once having coffee, al fresco, West Hollywood,
I noticed vibrations in my Fiestaware's
caffeinated surface, like schooled sperm—
chop, chop, chop, they circled above.
Midwestern militia groups think the helicopters
are from some secret force of allied governments.
Others say it's the FBI, CIA, or another dark intelligence.
I suspect a more plausible industrial conglomerate,
Dow, Phillip Morris, Nabisco, whose sole purpose . . . ?
They've increased their flights over my side of town,
their all-seeing lights split crowds gathered in parks.
They've influenced fashion designers to create neck braces
so we won't look up, big-brimmed hats like men in the Fifties.
I'm sure new building codes will be passed for glass roofs
and ceilings, rules against two-story homes.
I've told my lover to get off top of me
when I heard the timorous blades slice the air
like ninja swords lopping off genitalia
till we all look like Ken and Barbie, no nips or pubes.
The only thing we can do is celebrate Americana,
wave the flag, red, white, and blue,
pay tribute to our country's great leaders,

(mom, dad, and the kids will love it)
close ears to people's whining,
be afraid to vote.
My lover says I am paranoid,
his hand strokes to arouse me,
but I say listen to the thump, thump, thumping
coming closer like footsteps near a locked door,
the noise cresting to drown even the TV
and the lonely dissident voice lifted away.

SURVEILLANCE

MATHEWS HATED FAGS. He sat in a closed-up Winnebago, oppo-site the park, polishing his nightstick with a chamois. He watched the row of monitors—enhanced night vision—flash different camera an-gles: the johns, the fountains, a bus stop where no one ever gets on.

Ginger was the tech specialist. She made sure fresh videotape was being fed into the recorders. She listened to the sound pickups, reduc-ing any unnecessary noise. The boys in the department said Ginger did favors for her partners. Mathews dreamed about her dark nipples in his hands, while she begged for his cock.

Dorset knocked on the van, three quick taps, and stepped in. The six-foot Black officer was dressed in cruising drag. He wore ripped jeans, crotch padded (which he denied), and a body shirt that inde-cently exposed his chest. There was also a fake piercing on his left nipple. A silver arrow seemed to skewer the man's flesh and a small ser-pentine chain hung from the point to the quill. Dorset said, "Scoped the place. It's still too soon." He looked at each monitor; the blue-ness of the screens colored his eyes. He smirked, "Haven't done this park in a while; must be a whole new crop of clients just waiting to be picked up."

Mathews asked, "Anywhere you want to specialize?" Dorset looked at Mathews' pockmarked face, wondered why anybody so ugly would even care what homos did. For Dorset, he hated the idea that some guy was staring at his body, thinking about how it'd feel to fuck him. It was enough to turn Dorset's stomach against him.

Dorset said, "Yeah, I'll do the head. It's pretty safe and easy." That was Dorset's specialty back in South Bay. He'd once arrested seven men in one night, a bunch of fools. One guy complained that the cuffs were too tight. In rubber gloves, Dorset squeezed the cuffs tighter.

"Tell it to the ACLU, cocksucker!" Dorset got hand-slapped for wearing rubber gloves. No one could pin the handcuff part though. He got six weeks unpaid, but then again that's what the police leisure fund was for.

Dorset checked out Ginger's ass while she bent over the car radio. She whispered that they were starting surveillance recording. The dispatcher acknowledged and the radio went silent. Matthews put his nightstick on his crotch and pointed it up at Ginger. When Ginger turned around, the nightstick fell limp. Unknown to most people, Ginger's boyfriend was the department head who checked the authenticity of all video testimony/evidence. She actually made more money than Mathews and Dorset combined. Then again, most of the time they would have no case if it weren't for her.

In court, Ginger swore to the unbiased observations of her films. The jury trusted the slightly tall woman in the gray suit. The suit fit her body well, showing off her athletic firmness. The slew of attorneys was always polite to her. Her authoritative presence commanded respect. She would sit almost every afternoon in the small court theaters, filled with jury and judge. Every few minutes she would have to stop the videotape and, with a long wooden stick, tap on the screen identifying the suspect and officers involved. It was laborious for the jury since they sat on several cases at once in the same stuffy rooms for hours. A few people would be sickened, nearly choking, at the sight of two men negotiating sex.

Ginger's boyfriend would give her long midnight rubdowns. He would release the tense muscles down her neck to the back of her legs. She would gasp out loud at how one young officer went a little too far on a bust. She thought he needed some discipline. Ginger loved the feel of her boyfriend's strong grip on her wing-like muscled back, his soft palms smoothing her skin. He always promised he'd take care of it, and in a few days the young officer would be gone or demoted to a less prestigious department. Ginger's eyes would close to sleep, as her boyfriend lay like a heavy blanket on top of her body. His chest scratched into her.

Ten p.m. was when Mathews had wanted to start. He said a little prayer for the safety of his team because you never know when one of those faggots was crazy. Ginger checked the mics on Dorset one last time. When Dorset opened the door, the cool air invigorated Mathews. It made his adrenaline rush through his body a little more quickly, a little more sweetly.

The cool air scented with pine reminded Mathews of back home, Lake Hillsburg. He worked the summers on the lake. His father owned a little motel along the beach. Skiers after a long day, their bodies covered in suntan lotion, would pay his father to use the wooden stalls on their property. Mathews would lead them outside the office past electric fan noises and the slap of the screen door. Mathews would carry their towel, a bar of soap and a green plastic key ring that said, "Hillsburg MMM . . . Motel." His mother ran the coffee shop. He'd unlock the two-sectioned stall, half dressing room, the rest a wood-slatted shower. Mathews would step inside the shower, his palm testing the temperature and ask how they liked it.

When Mathews was sixteen, one of the guys, a tall blond who was slightly hairy, had really taken to Mathews. He wanted to know Mathews' first name, what he did for fun; if Mathews wanted to stay, they could take a late walk around the lake. Mathews waited outside the shower, sitting on the weathered bench, once painted green. His father showed the last of the customers to the stalls himself, his thongs clapping the bottom of his feet and the trail of stones.

The guy came out, half dripping. He wore bright yellow trunks and the motel's white towel around his neck. He held both ends of the towel with his hands. Mathews stared at the Japanese fish tattoo on the guy's arm. It looked like it could swim away, as the guy nervously twisted the towel.

Mathews walked a few feet ahead, kicking driftwood along the shore, not really saying anything. The guy followed anyway. The sun drowned itself at the far end of the lake and a magenta oil slick seemed to follow them. By the time they got to the other side, it was night; Mathews could see lights strung up like Christmas on the motel's dock. The tall man came up behind Mathews gently. His fur-covered forearms held him up. Big hands slid up and down Mathews' chest, sometimes patting to see how firm his chest and stomach were. One hand had slipped inside Mathews' trunks. He wanted to spasm, wanted to push away as the stranger grabbed his balls tightly, then started to stroke his erection. Mathews twisted as the other hand went up his shirt and pulled at his nipples, as if he was a woman. He then felt himself come, the wet netting of his trunks sticking to his skin. The stranger's lips rested on Mathew's ear, whispering, "Do you want more?" Mathews ran away, getting caught up in twigs, low branches and tree roots that lashed out and grabbed his feet. He hid in the one empty motel room. He kept the lights off as the moon dripped off the curtains and pooled underneath the door. He could hear his father screaming his name, "Jack? Jack!"

Dorset was a pro, inconspicuous if he wanted to be. He was perfect bait. He'd learned to be a chameleon in a gay bar around his parents' home. One moment he was a wallflower, the next everyone's phone fantasy come to life. He hypnotized with the help of dance music, flashing lights, and alcohol. He would collect partners and see how many drinks he could bum off them, or packs of cigarettes. When the partner would be insistent on taking Dorset home, either by tugging on Dorset's arm or rubbing his inner thigh, Dorset would agree. He'd walk out amicably, saying goodnight to the bartenders or doorman. Outside, the muffled beat of a music video mixed with the slow tread of a parking car. The partner would try to hug Dorset as he started to light a cigarette. If the guy got too close, Dorset would flick the cigarette at him. He'd try to get the smoldering butt inside the front of his shirt, or in a loose pocket. The guy would stumble back confused as Dorset climbed into his 4x4, nearly backing into him, almost breaking a few ribs, puncturing his heart.

Lt. Dorset circled the park. There was no way for Mathews to contact Dorset directly by radio. The faggots had learned to detect a prowler, especially when the prowler talked out loud to himself. Fairies disappear at the first sign of trouble. What the department had developed was a kind of radio beeper. It looked like a watch, but instead of beeping, it sent a painless thump. The device was heralded as an improvement in police protection. The codes were set. One thump meant go to the johns, two meant fountain, three bus stop, four home.

To Dorset, every park smelled the same at night; the odor of a passing bum, beer on wet grass, urinals, and Lysol. Dorset knew about parks when he was a kid. A whole group of guys after school would get in Dorset's pickup. They'd drive over to Central, with the stereo cranking, the bass pumping. The guys would fly out the sides, rush into a men's room before any faggot could even begin to pull up his pants. The guys would all laugh, running out of the head, yelling, "Cocksuckers, pussyboys!" It was still early enough for other people to be around, all staring at the two queers. Embarrassed, the men would slink away, hoping no one recognized them, the daylight striking their faces.

On one monitor, Mathews observed the john being occupied by one male Caucasian, loitering around the urinals. Ginger sent one pulse to Dorset's "thumper." Dorset took his sweet pokey time so as not to alarm any unseen sex offenders. When Dorset finally arrived, the suspect had been standing there with a raging hard-on that Dorset had to comment on. Ginger told Mathews, "I'm getting great reception!" Mathews smiled at her enthusiasm.

The suspect told Dorset, "How about sucking it?"

Dorset said, "No way, man. Aren't you afraid you'll infect someone?"

The guy said, "I'm clean. I won't shoot in your mouth." That was all Mathews needed.

He sent Dorset a four-thump signal. Dorset gave the suspect a look that said you been had. Fortunately, the cameras were facing the wrong way. All the tapes would show is Dorset turning on his heels. The suspect now had a warrant for his arrest. At any time, the police could come calling, at work, school, family, anywhere. With the help of the FBI, intimidating red letters would be mailed to them, citations that warned of the results of failure to appear in court at a certain time and date. Sometimes a local newspaper would run photographs with names and addresses of accused HIV criminals, "Found Promoting Unsafe and Risky Sex." Most people agreed with the House Speaker's beliefs on HIV, echoing his words, "Anyone (gay) attempting unsafe or risky sex was a harm to society as a whole, damaging the social and economic balance of the greater nation."

It was Mathews' turn when Dorset came back. Mathews slipped his club into the "o" ring at his backside. He took his long leather trench coat off the headrest of the front seat. Mathews was head-to-toe in black; only his face seemed to catch light. It was marked by shadow scars from when he had chickenpox.

Mathews knew he was good-looking at sixteen. It wasn't the first time that some guy wanted to do him. It was just that he'd never let anyone touch him before. It scared him to have hands on his body. At home his father wouldn't even touch him; his mother only gave quick pecks to his cheeks.

When the chickenpox came, he knew he shouldn't be out of bed. He just wanted a moment of fresh air. He lay on the hammock at the front of the motel; no one was around. Everyone was still on the lake. His father came up the steps with a customer and, through sleepy eyes, Mathews could see it was the guy from the shower. His father, a big fellow in a red plaid shirt, started yelling at Mathews to get back in bed before he got worse. Mathews didn't move right away. The man didn't seem to recognize him, didn't even look his way. The man came back outside the office, having just paid his bill. He looked at Mathews, still on the hammock, and took a deep breath, staring at the mountains, exclaiming, "I do love this place!! I love coming back year after year." Mathews stared at the man. He turned back to Mathews and said, "God look at those marks, must be really bad," The man touched his chin. "I remember when I had chickenpox. You better not scratch." Then in a whisper, "They may ruin your skin."

By the end of the night, Mathews' team rounded up five HIV criminals. The only questionable incident was when Mathews went for one more bust at the head. Surveillance teams rarely took a place more than one time and never arrested since they had such a backlog of HIV; they kept files instead. Dorset sat back in a bucket seat, resting a bit, thinking about sleep. Ginger watched as a young man on his knees slipped a condom on Mathews' dick. He eagerly began to suck. Ginger sent a four-thump signal to Mathews, but he ignored it. Ginger didn't really care; she knew Mathews would slip her a twenty tonight. She fed some blank action video, shot earlier, into the recorder. With the new flying erase heads, anything was possible on tape. She began to shut down the sets, preparing to go.

When Mathews asked the young man if he wanted to get fucked, and he said yes, Mathews flung back his leather coat. He swung his night stick like a cock against a face. The blood was lubrication on the floor. With a latex finger, Mathews wrote, "The only Good Homo is a Dead Homo." The letters were bold and started to seep into the tile's cracked grout.

VI

I worry who will love him after I am gone.

"HEROES"

Editors' note: We believe these pages are the beginning of a novel or novella that was left unfinished when Cuadros died. Because the literary quality is high, because the work explores his experience in the last couple of years of his life, and because his moving into long-form prose signals the work we might have seen from him had he lived, we have chosen to include it in this collection.

I.

I LET THE shower run hot over my back till it hurts just a little, the skin tensing, muscles irritable then surrendering. Steam rises in the tub around my large feet and toes, swaddles my calves and thighs. In clouds, the vapor lifts toward the cell-like window, out through the screen to a cooler freedom. I imagine that the moon hovers like a voyeur, observing my movements, watching intensely my more intimate procedures. My hand cups warm water under my scrotum, splashes against my anus.

The face of the moon appears unchanging tonight, its crater eyes peer through the pittosporum tree's branches, laden with small white flowers. The flowers exude a thick, oily aroma that buries Fountain Avenue. I lift my arm as if to push aside those branches, a violent summer wind myself, shamelessly exposing the voyeur. I rub clear blackberry soap in the pits of my arms, washing away the odor that has built up during the hundred-and-six-degree day. The wiriness of my pubic hair traps globes of lather as I clean the shaft of my dick. The folds of skin around my balls smell of my body's unctuous sweat, a medicinal odor, metallic from the various medications meant to protect my one remaining T-cell.

My chest, back, and neck shiver uncontrollably in the shower. At first, I assume it is somehow my body at fault, that I have caught some new illness, carelessly presented myself to an airborne virus that will eventually kill me. It is moments before I notice the shower's water temperature has suddenly plummeted. I continue to clean after I've adjusted the faucet. Pumice is embedded in the bar of soap; the head of my cock, the crack of my ass tingle with the abrasion.

I stick a tentative finger in my asshole, afraid my finger might come out with shit or my asshole explode diarrhea. I press a little past the sphincter; I will the muscle to relax, then tighten again. My body obeys. With both hands I rub the bar of soap quickly between palms. With one hand I start to pull on my dick; with my other hand, I spread open my cheeks, again pushing my middle finger inside my ass, loosening the muscle then placing another finger beside.

All my sex fantasies begin with my being owned by an older white man, a large-chested man, gray-haired, an intelligent writer of essays and opinions, someone not afraid to put bruises on my body or to kiss me on the lips, his arms pulling me in a suffocating embrace. I read *Mr. Benson* at the age of twenty-one, reciting it to my sex partners before bedtime; some were too embarrassed by its explicitness, asking me to take the book home when I left their apartment. I imagine my Mister _____ grabbing my balls and hard dick, pulling them roughly out from behind me toward my own asshole, my cock straining from its stiffness, him slamming my face up against the shower walls, his hand pressing down where neck and spine meet. He calls me by my first name, the shortened version because he thinks it's more masculine. His voice conveys anger, excitement, pleasure, or tenderness just by the way he says Gil.

When he cums he howls like a bloodthirsty animal under the full moon, waking timid neighbors too afraid to pound the common connecting walls of our apartments. They think of limbs and torso bruised, a spouse with blackened eyes, a lover stabbed repeatedly, a dark man jailed for his rage, released into a quiet, ignorant neighborhood. They hear the crack of his hand against my ass, my scream he muffles with his fist as he shoves his still stiff and cum-dripping cock into my hole. He says he loves his white dick up my dark-brown ass. My hand stops jerking for a moment, my body spasms as I turn in the shower and the tin-tasting water runs into my mouth. The moon moves away from the window.

I wipe my body with sun-dried towels fetched from the clothes-line out back; the black towels are stiff and scratchy. The ends I grab like a shoe-polishing rag and rub across my back, down my legs, finger in between toes. The towels are now slightly damp; they smell of detergent and my flesh. I swab the bathroom mirror, one moment showing a blur of brown skin, black hair, then through clear bands on the glass I can see my eyes, large white saucers surrounding dark maple orbs. Above my pierced nipple is a scar shaped like an animal's paw, pink and raised. I touch it more gently than any other part of my body; I'm still afraid that the skin where the Hickman catheter had been might break open like a sacred heart. It was a simple procedure to remove the attachment—local anesthesia, a clipping of the surgical thread that tied the white tube to a secure part of skin. Afterwards the doctor withdrew the long white tube that led into my heart. He asked if I could feel the Hickman being extracted. I said, "Not really." What I did feel was a small sensation where the doctor placed his cold, latex-covered hands near the opening, a numb feeling of the insides of my chest being rubbed by the small bulbous ending.

For months I had the Hickman. The infusions I had to take while fighting the cryptococcal meningitis wrecked my veins; regular IVs were hard to put in. I'd fought against the Hickman, uncomfortable with this added jewelry.

Hickmans used to mean certain death. Soon. My first lover died just after he had one installed. The doctors convinced me to sign papers to allow the procedure, telling me how much easier it would be for John's veins, and all the while I kept on thinking how ugly his broad chest would look from now on, freakish. Staring at my own scarred chest, I think that I am the first person I know who survived one and had it removed. I imagine an invisible tube sewn onto my chest, the other end attached to John; I am too afraid to pull away and tear our skin, and all I can think is, he is dead.

I dry under my arms, notice as I raise them that there is a bulkiness I'm not used to, my shoulders and lats larger than yesterday. My body changes shape rapidly. Before the meningitis, I weighed close to two hundred pounds, all fat for my five-foot-six-inch body. While I stayed in the hospital, the medications caused me to shit endlessly till it was no longer controllable, my bowel movements pure liquid. My weight dropped steadily, and for the first time in my life I was underweight, one hundred and thirty-eight. I began to fit into clothes I had always wanted to, excitedly having to try things on at least three times to find the right smaller size. My stomach showed the muscles that make the abdomen, the curving lines that lead to my crotch. Every time I passed a mirror it was like a new person was there, and I liked him much more, how small and unassuming he'd become, even a bit sexier than I remember him ever being.

My skin had changed color too, slightly orange from a MAC prophylactic medication I took. My fevers subsided, the mycobacterium having been reduced. People constantly stopped me on the streets or in the stores asking where I was from, staring at my glowing skin. The black tattoo designs slipping out from under my short-sleeve shirts suggested the Middle East, Turkey, India. They would be amused by my answer—California. They would speak slowly to me as if English wasn't my first language. "No, really, where are your parents from? Grandparents?"

I flex my arm in the mirror and impress myself. The steroids I've been taking are working; their only drawback, the possibility of encouraging a cancerous growth. The diarrhea is slightly controlled by a twice-daily injection of another drug. I turn to look at my backside, my flattened, saggy AZT butt is now growing round and firm again. I believe all the risks are worth it.

Marcus sits splay-legged on the floor, his large tablet of watercolor paper in front of him. He uses a pencil to fill in some small details in the background of a portrait he's done of me; lush green leaves grow out directly from the surface. The TV's glow makes the white paper change hues; on the screen, flesh is blurred pink and spotty, a dick pumping into a shaved white ass, a prison scene in a lower metal bunk bed. The stereo is also on, what I left as I went into the shower. A Bowie CD shuffles, then the opening sounds of electronic violins, whining and cold. I notice on Marcus's thigh a small mark, darker than a bruise, lighter than a birthmark. It was what had started the small fight between us—me not understanding why his doctor wouldn't biopsy the spot right away, Marcus telling me how uncaring County hospital is, how it does not compare with my private insurance. His real concern is the pain he feels, a numbness shooting up his calves, concentrating in his knees. He says his doctors don't believe he's in that much pain, that because he's on Medi-Cal/Medicare (or, as we call it, Medi-apathy) they won't prescribe anything stronger than Tylenol with codeine. For something stronger, he would have to pay for the prescription himself. He asks me, "With what money?"

Marcus rubs his legs like an old man, says, "Fuck," under his breath. His fingers run over what I fear is the beginning of lesions covering his body. I try not to let the two-centimeter mark, the color of red-and-blue melted candle wax, upset me too much again. I wonder, are there cancerous growths hidden in the walls of his lungs, the surface of his brain? Will he be one of the ones who go quickly? There is nothing I can do for him. I am not his doctor. If I could, I would buy him health insurance, would change the whole world so that it would be I who died first. It comforts me to think he will survive after I've gone; he is the part of me that will continue. I don't want to believe anything else except I worry who will love him after I am gone; will he become as bitter and lonely as I became after John died? Will he take care of himself, or let everything fall apart?

John's death is still close enough that I can feel the thought change the muscles in my face, my cheeks tighten, the corners of my mouth frown. Marcus looks up, tilts his head at my expression, trying to decipher what I am thinking. I want to release him, to end this relationship before either one of us gets sicker. Bowie sings in the impassioned and crestfallen tone that I feel.

> *Though nothing, nothing will keep us together.*
> *We can beat them, forever and ever.*
> *Oh we can be heroes, just for one day . . .*

I slide underneath the striped black-and-white sheets of my bed, my warm skin touching the cool fabric with my toes. I curl onto my side facing the TV screen and recognize the video Marcus is playing. The story is about a speed trap on a highway in the South. Truckers and buff young hitchhikers often use the road, pulling over to the side to fuck in the back of big rigs. After they've just cummed, patrolmen bang with nightsticks on the metal back doors, calling them "homos, queers!" Large muscular arms are pulled back and handcuffed, while the merchandise in the trucks is confiscated.

The men are forced into a *Cool Hand Luke*–type labor camp where blond boys are forcibly raped and the largest-dicked man is in perpetual solitary confinement, frustrated he can't get it on with the other inmates or guards. The truth of the video appears that the reason for his confinement is his lack of a full and useful erection.

Marcus sits back and finishes the last swigs of beer in his glass. I have lost count of his drinking tonight, slightly glad of this freedom of mind. His mustache catches small droplets of fluid on the tips. He comes over to me in bed after he's put his painting away. My dick stiffens a little, another side effect of the testosterone steroid. I think of his dick hardening and then sitting on it, but I fear liquid shit covering the bedsheets, his dick, and my ass. His face moves close to mine, and then he kisses me. His mouth is wet and tastes of beer and the cold ice cubes he places in his glass. My father drank warm beer from cans he stored in the garage, so to me Marcus's habit of putting ice in his beer seems luxurious. The TV is flickering the last scenes of the video, the guards and inmates in a final orgy. Marcus reaches under the sheets in the bed, grabs the hair of my crotch roughly. I return his kisses, biting fully his lower lip, not wanting to extract blood but feeling compelled to. It becomes a contest of who will wince first. He turns his hand, fingers twined in the hair. I let go of his lip, afraid I'll bite through. He holds on. His tongue sidles down my torso and he lifts my legs up. I start to push away, can tell he wants to eat my ass. He turns me on my knees and I can feel his tongue pressing into my hole and again I move away. I can hear Marcus sigh in frustration. I look over at the screen and see a man squatting over two cocks. Marcus slips his white T-shirt off and I pull his boxers down over his ass. His dick is musty next to my nose. He says, "You're all clean and I'm dirty." I tell him I like it that way. The tip of his dick is moist with urine. I lick at the small droplet, let my tongue linger in the small slot at the head of his penis. Somehow the camera shows the man's asshole expanding to fit the two dicks. I lift the weight of Marcus's limp and growing cock with my tongue. Again, I breathe in deeply. I take his dick all the way into my mouth, putting my hand at the base, willing it to become hard by trapping pressure. Marcus responds with deep-throated moans, sighs. It doesn't seem to take long to suck him off, my mouth enjoying the work it's performing, my hands curved around Marcus's thighs. The video screen hisses a snowfield, the end of the tape. His fluid lies over my tongue, salty and full of potential life. It invades my body like love.

I am in my old home in Pasadena, in the bathtub. The walls around the tub crumble plaster into tepid water. I am slightly surprised when John's hand moves to the water faucet letting the tub fill with more warm water, silky with baking soda. I smell shit, the kind of shit John had while he was sick in the hospital. The smell at once overwhelms then dissipates as I look into his face, his blue eyes. In his eyes I see myself much younger and naïve. My face looks less haggard, smooth and without care, college my only concern. John looks as he did, young again, his cheeks full and ruddy, his blond hair neatly combed to the side. On his ring finger, a small gold wedding band, one of a pair we had exchanged at Christmas. The gold glimmers as his hand squeezes a sea sponge. The texture of the sponge is not rough, but soapy as he runs it over my arm, not yet tattooed; water trickles as tears would. I imagine I can taste the bitterness of the water.

I begin to cry as I notice the sponge moving over small raised marks on my skin. The odd-shaped badges are dark as bruises and covered with thread-like red veins. I try to pick on one, to dig out the imperfection with my nail. John holds my hand steady, doesn't let me finish what I've started. A trickle of blood oozes from under the scar. As it hits the water, the color widens like melted wax dripping into a warm pool. The blood floats like thin petals of lotus flowers on the surface, constantly moving and in flux. The blooms land on my legs and permanently mark those areas.

John says, "Try not to cry." And I fail. Embarrassed at my weakness, I sink underneath the water and all sound is muffled. I shake my head under the water, come up for air gasping like a young boy. I smell gasoline, the sulfur from a match. Around the tub's ledge are votive candles. Under the showerhead and the chrome enema hose is a crucifix of Jesus. Red oil drips from the small marks in his forehead, palms, and feet. As his blood touches the water, steam plumes upward like lava flowing into the ocean. The marks on my legs and arms fall away in the water; they become rose petals. John tells me if I drain the water, he can read the future by the petals lying in the tub. I stand up and Marcus is there now, naked with a large bath sheet. He pats me dry. I kiss him but he turns away, which only makes me more determined to bite through his lips. Marcus turns back into John and then John disappears. The towel floats invisibly, held by open arms.

2.

I stand before a billboard-size drawing of a severed head or skull done in graffiti fashion, as if the artist had used the four colors available to him from a multicolored click ballpoint pen, the kind stores sell during back-to-school sales. I move a small medallion of Saint Lazarus along a metal bead chain I am wearing, contemplating how something as mundane and unremarkable could be next to a Barbara Kruger installation. Then I notice the Robert Longo paintings. Oh, I say to myself.

I can hear the soles of Kevin's shoes stepping toward me on the hardwood floor of the gallery. They stop next to me, looking where I'm looking. Kevin then says with a certain amount of phlegm stuck in his throat, "Uh, I can't stand his work." I smile broadly. Together we move over to the Cindy Sherman photos. One especially strikes me, almost life-size. She has done a self-portrait modeled on a well-known late Renaissance painting of a woman with a man's severed head on a silver platter. For some reason, I couldn't remember the name of the famous painting and its theme. I could only remember the woman had to kill the man.

I call over to Kevin who is chuckling at the visible straps used in another Sherman photograph that holds a body mold of breasts over Sherman's body. I tell Kevin in a sideways manner they sell those kinds of things at the Pleasure Chest: butts, penises, vaginas.

Kevin looks over at me thoughtfully, studying my face, and I become nervous. He moves with determined steps and grabs my jaw, turns my face under one of the overhanging lights. He brushes at my beard, moving the hair out of the way so he could see the skin underneath more clearly. Teeth marks. Kevin then lifts my arm, turns it slightly. Again, he studies it carefully, touching the large bruise gently.

"What's going on?" he asks.

I look into his eyes and see something that I had once loved long ago and then I turn away, a bit ashamed and terrified. "Marcus just got a little carried away."

"Oh," Kevin said matter-of-factly, also now slightly embarrassed.

I concentrate on the prosthetic nipple aiming out between fine silk garments, a stream of milk shooting out from the tip. "It didn't hurt."

Kevin moves my face to his. At first, I think he is going to kiss me. Instead, he inspects my lower lip, a scab of blood nearby. Standing so close to him, like when we were lovers, I notice now how large his body has become, how his arms are heavy with muscle and his chest seems made of steel plates. I marvel how dedicated he has been with his weight training. I tell him in a confidential manner, "Marcus feels a lot of insecurity when you are around me."

Kevin scans my body for more evidence, asks, "Why?"

With deadpan delivery, I tell him, "How would you like the ex-wife hanging around all the time?"

"Is that what he's worried about, you and I getting back together?"

I tell Kevin, "Not a chance, huh?"

Kevin shakes his head.

While Kevin fixes dinner in the kitchen, I sit in the living room in his chair, thumbing through a new *Drummer* magazine. Its cover story, "Fag Skin Heads: the Leather Community's Next Generation." Kevin yells from the kitchen, "There's an article on Ron Athey inside."

I tell him I found it already.

In the article, an old leather fag interviews Ron about how Ron feels doing body piercing, a kind of artwork. He talks of the nineteen-year-old "bottomless pit" he fucks with, nothing really about Ron's performance art work or aesthetics. There are just some old, tired lines offered I'm sure by the journalist about Modern Primitives. The pictures show various shots of Ron's tattooed body, even his dick with Christ done in English calligraphy. I laugh at the thought that I might be a Modern Primitive in the making, more really a trendy/ Provincial.

I had taken Marcus to hear Ron read some of his literary work at A Different Light bookstore. The place was packed with people, one with bright purple hair, also a Black male I knew Ron used in his performance work. Marcus looked around, then at me. "I'm the oldest one here." I pointed to a much older man sitting at the other side. Marcus seemed somewhat relieved, his less-than-current salt-and-pepper goatee, his tight-fitting 501s and white T-shirt looking a bit dated compared to the black-clad, pierced-eyebrow crowd. Ron read stories of his upbringing: strict, religious, and perverted. The stories always took turns that really disturbed me, places I was afraid of but wasn't interested in staying in either. I kept on thinking what about the sister; what happened to her after all these forced enemas, did the gospel singer ever again have a full stigmata, or was it all lies in the first place? Deep inside, I wondered if Ron had ever made love to little boys as a little boy himself, or did he just want to hurt them?

When the reading was over, I rushed out of the bookstore, afraid I'd meet Ron. I was afraid I'd have to lie and tell him I liked the stories a lot, when really I wanted to question the choices he made in his storytelling. Marcus followed me, running across the street to catch the shuttle bus home, not understanding why I didn't want to say hello to Ron at least.

At my apartment, I lit three candles and a bowl of sage and smudged the four directions in each of my rooms. Marcus lay on the bed, his hands behind his head, legs crossed and pushing the bulge that was between his legs. I played a CD of Tibetan monks chanting "Om" and rang a brass meditation bowl I picked up in Chinatown. Whatever may have followed me home from the reading, I was sure, was truly killed. Marcus looked at me, his green eyes animalistic, a hypnotist or snake charmer. I stepped out of my shoes, pulled my socks and shirt off. With one movement I shucked off my pants and underwear. The lights were on, so I walked to the switch. I told Marcus I would be right back. In the bathroom, I pulled a cold washcloth across my ass, sticking a finger inside as one would to clean an ear. Afterwards I splashed cinnamon and clove oil on my skin. It made me feel warm, as if I was wearing a heated robe. I sat by Marcus and undid his belt and the buttons of his jeans. I pulled out his dick from his boxers and began to suck. I then straddled his face, still sucking his dick. His hand spread my cheeks open. I didn't care that I wasn't particularly clean or that I might smell of shit and sweat. I just wanted to suck Marcus off until he came. Marcus's hand moved slowly, feeling the edges of my asshole, his tongue flickering the undersides of my balls. I could feel his breathing. He moved my ass lower till my dick was in his mouth. He told me to piss a little. With a bit of concentration, I let out a small amount, not sure that I could easily control the stream if it started. He began to make a gagging noise and at once I realized my piss tasted of all the medications I took. I was glad I hadn't continued pissing. Without warning, he turned me over till I was the one on the bottom, his dick fully hard and choking. With a little pause he began to piss, a little trickle at first but then a strong stream. I didn't ask for it, but he gave it anyway. He tasted of beer and it was watery. I thought the fluid would overflow my mouth but as soon as it started, I was sad it finished, and I began to suck hard for more. With my ass in the air, his arms hooked under my knees, Marcus spit into his hand. I could smell his own sweaty ass at my nose, could feel his fingers working next to my ass, a small jab of his finger and then more spit, more fingers.

Kevin and I lie on his bed, having finished dinner. Earlier that evening, we had given each other steroid shots in the ass. It always made me feel funny how he'd drop his pants to the floor, protrude his rump out from the sink he leaned against. I would only expose a small portion of my ass, pulling my underwear down so far, tying up my shirt around my chest. He would warn me, "You'll feel a little stick." Where I would just wipe with an alcohol swab, then jab till the amber fluid was completely pressed out of the injection tube. I'm always a bit nervous pulling out the needle, though, afraid blood might erupt wildly, that it would splash in my eyes or open mouth. I notice a little blood runs out in a tiny trickle on Kevin's ass. I open another alcohol swab and dab at it. I look at the small square cloth; the blood has made an interesting blot. I imagine a dragon, wings spread open in outrage, its head turned to the right and ready to spew fire from its mouth. I looked at it for a long time. Kevin had already pulled his pants back up, his briefs that proclaim "Calvin Klein, Calvin Klein . . ." around the waistband.

Kevin turns the VCR to play and props pillows up on the headboard. He is down to his briefs and so am I, except I wear a T-shirt too, while Kevin is bare-chested. I tell him Marcus, whom I had just called on the telephone, knew that I was going to spend the night here, as if by psychic fortune-telling. Kevin shrugs. I say, "I guess I'd worry too if I was Marcus. He always mentions how you took care of me while I was sick with the meningitis. The truth is I don't even remember it."

Kevin agrees, says, "It's because you were really sick and mentally out of it."

I ask timidly, "How long ago?"

Kevin says, "Only a year. You kept on calling me, saying that voices were going off in your head. That your parents were berating you. You even thought they wanted to kill you. The pain must have been enormous. You walked around as if your head wasn't attached to your body, like it would fall off."

I tell Kevin, "I really want to remember it, but it's like I was Lazarus, raised by you from the dead." With a pause I then ask Kevin, "How can I get him not to worry about us getting back together; I mean, we're sleeping together but we're not having sex."

Kevin fast-forwards the video, says, "He'll just have to see by our actions. It just goes to show you he doesn't trust himself that much; why should he trust us?"

I ask, "What should I do?"

Kevin slows down the video to normal speed, "You can only work on yourself. Be concerned about how you feel. If you feel love for him, it's because it's a reflection of the love you have for yourself." The video plays a black-and-white movie. It shows a laboratory, a haughty scientist, an old Black woman, a drunken white woman. They go to Africa; he is looking for a youth-restoring drug the old Black woman has told him about. In this tribe the old Black woman is restored to youth due to the sacrifice of a young Black male. They give the white woman any wish she'd like because they are going to have to kill her since she knows the secret to the restoring power. She wishes that they sacrifice her husband, the scientist; that way she will be young again. I can feel my own breath slowing down as the woman looks into a mirror; my arms tingle with sleepiness while she runs the back of her palms softly over the curves of her cheeks.

I dream of Marcus working in the garden in front of a house we have just bought. It is overrun with jungle vines, plants, and roots. Marcus has to dig up all the foliage in order to re-landscape the property. He is angry at all the mess, the half-dug holes in the soil, the way the bougainvillea have covered the trellis on the front porch, making it warp and bend. I notice that small animals seem to show up wounded and hurt. Marcus lifts them to a work table and bandages the injured legs and wings. The small animals seem grateful, trusting and happy near Marcus. He is also smiling, but is angry, I can see, at whoever did such mean things to animals and plants. Some of these native plants, he tells me, can't be found in nurseries anymore. A prehistoric porcupine lumbers near his feet. With gloved hands Marcus picks it up. He asks me, shouldn't I be ready for the funeral?

All at once I remember the funeral I am supposed to be at. I am dressed in a dark blue suit and tie. I walk over the hill and see people moving toward the beach to where the funeral is being held. Kevin is the one they are going to bury. At first, I feel as if I should be hysterical, crying uncontrollably, but I'm not. There is calmness in my heart, my hands steady as I hold them out in front of me.

Stairs lead downward to the beach. Everyone is moving toward the right-hand stairs. I get annoyed with the crowd. I move to the stairs on the left, can see they cross back and forth with three different rows of stairs. I step down, uninterested in walking that many stairs, so I take two, then three steps at a time. Then I'm floating down the stairs, not even walking at all. As I float toward the bottom, I see Kevin making his way up. He stops and marvels at my ability to float.

He then challenges me, asks, how high can I go? I float up to his shoulders; then he says, how low? At first, I hesitate, not sure of my ability. I concentrate, push my body down till it almost touches. It is far harder to do this and be in control. My happiness moves away.

Kevin looks at a person in a direction I can't see but somehow know he's talking to Marcus. Kevin tells Marcus, "See that?" I can't feel a thing of what Marcus replies.

3.

Marcus is quiet, moving tersely about his bleak apartment, which is filled with a turned-over wicker basket for a table, blankets on the floor for the bed, an old TV sitting precarious on sagging moving boxes, a few large wilting plants lacking sufficient sunlight. Underneath the window a row of paperback autobiographies—Gilda Radner, Gloria Vanderbilt, *Call Me Anna* by Patty Duke, and *Poor Little Rich Girl* by Barbara Hutton. Marcus slams down pill bottles of Dapsone and Diflucan on the kitchen counter, taking out a few of each kind and placing the tablets and other capsules in his pocket pill cases. He wrestles the last assortment out of a punchcard dispenser for a university study to help prevent the development of blindness.

I light a menthol cigarette from a pack he's left on the love sofa given to him by a lesbian friend's lover. On the armrest a dinner plate from an old set I had given him is filled with cigarette stubs, a few coagulated fries from the burger stand around the corner, and ashes. I let the smoke fill my lungs, exhale toward the ceiling in a sharp burst. I sense that he's mad at me for some reason to do with Kevin.

On the floor, near my feet, are music tapes Marcus has been listening to. Most are old 1970s disco and other later dance music. Often when I'm working on bills, writing letters to my friends, or reading a magazine, Marcus puts on his earphones and plays his music. I can hear the steady rhythm and tempo, the thump of the bass just loud enough for me to hear, escaping from the small, cushioned speakers. Sometimes I can see Marcus lift his hands in the air, twisting and turning his wrists, flexing his fingers as if in dance or as Norma Desmond descending her staircase in the movie *Sunset Boulevard*, playing in demented reverie her Salome, her return.

It's when he notices that I am watching him he'll turn off his music with a click and ask, "What?"

"Nothing," I'll answer, "just watching you." He'll again turn on his music without his hands moving in the air. I go back to my letter writing, my sealing of envelopes and pasting stamps, disappointed as if I popped a delicate multicolored soap bubble floating in solitude across a park on a gentle wind.

It's his form of meditation, I've determined; he always looks refreshed, the lines in his face smoothed after listening to a hour or so of Stephanie Mills, Patti Austin, and even Donna Summer's *Once Upon a Time*. Afterwards, he tells me stories of the past, before the disease, when he went to discos and worked and had more than enough money, being in charge of a large nursery that catered to the movie industry, and always invited out to the bars and clubs. Blacks, whites, and Latinos shared the dance floor then, and everywhere reeked of poppers making hearts beat harder; people were generous in sharing their drugs, and if you wanted to fuck some guy or couple of guys you just went up to them and said, Let's go fuck. Marcus gets this sort of Allen Ginsberg smile as if reciting poetry about Armageddon, peyote, and the individual arms of Shiva.

I had missed the disco era, being somewhat younger than Marcus's forty years. We joked in school how disco wasn't dead, it just smelled funny. Cliques formed around different styles of music; doing drugs was a given in any of the high school groups. The bottom line was your music was your identity. My sophomore year, the King and Queen of the prom were photographed in the annual in this tango pose, him wearing flared polyester pants and open shirt with gold chain, her dress slit up to her waist. My senior year the King wore a ripped-up T-shirt held together with safety pins, and the Queen a traditional prom dress with properly coiffed hair. Even though no one voted for her, she was crowned queen. It was the Reagan era. Everyone was supposed to vote for Steve Allison, the biggest queen on campus, who would wear short-short cut-off jeans, sit on the ground, and let his dick fall out. He'd exclaim in gym, "Oh my, she fell out!," making all the jocks groan with disgust. Again, it was the Reagan era. Going to discos meant you were somehow a part of the establishment, even though my age group would never use the word "establishment" ourselves. We thought it was what older kids did when they lost touch of what was cool and weren't invited to slam dance or pogo at the clubs like the Whiskey, Roxy, or Troubadour.

Marcus goes through the tapes on the floor, placing the cassettes into their cases, putting a few into his backpack. He then waters his plants with a large bottle filled with a bluish liquid. He has told me how he was the best in his business, that people were always amazed at his ability to nurture plants, the lushness of his nursery; bitingly, he jokes how plants are easier to have relationships with. "They ask for so little and give so much in return." Marcus lifts a small ceramic pot up to the light. It's a pineapple he's planted. He's told me how when he worked for the nursery, he'd plant a few in decorative pots, and people would be in awe, thinking it was a rare and exotic plant, wanting desperately to purchase the find. He'd then tell them it was just a pineapple. A stem would reach upward, the leaves changing colors from purple to orange, and the small bulbous end would swell, expand, and elongate like a small hand grenade or a fist rising on the dance floor, fingers opening, blooming under a mirrored ball spinning in the sky and called simply the sun.

Marcus stands in front of me, in jeans that seem a little too baggy for him, the new style. He lifts his backpack over his shoulder, spins his keys on his finger, sighs that he's ready to go.

When we arrive at the food bank, I can sense Marcus's neck muscles tighten, his face becoming stone-like, his body's movements stiff and military. We walk up to the reception desk in the dark corner of the lobby. A fresh-faced young lesbian hands us a sticker with the word "Visitor" printed boldly. Marcus keeps the sticker pasted to his finger and walks across the lobby toward the large room where the food bank is. I place the sticker on my jeans pocket, afraid like Marcus that the sticker's glue will stain my shirt. That's where we've been told to place our tags numerous times, stopped in the hallways by security guards. We've complained every time how it damages our clothes, how we can't afford to be buying new clothes all the time on Social Security. As we pass a trash can, Marcus tosses in the folded-over visitor label, mumbling, "Fuck their rules."

The room is packed. The twenty-odd tables are filled with men and women sitting around reading magazines, most just staring into space, biding their time till their name is called and their groceries are pulled from unseen shelves in the warehouse. Everyone seems to be wearing the visitor tags where they're supposed to, on the right shirt pocket, the day's date penned in with a thick black marker giving them the look of being processed for a concentration camp. Feeble arms and hands place the single-sheet paperwork necessary to getting the food into a black painted box. A sign nearby states, "Don't ask questions." Another: "Don't make requests."

Marcus sits farthest away from the group. Every time we come here, he tells me how he used to volunteer. "But that was before they stopped having clients work here because they would steal food for themselves or give their friends extras." He says he used to know most of the men coming in, having tricked with them at one time or from when he went to AA. With an open palm, he says, "Now," scanning the room for a familiar face, someone from the days when he really felt a part of a community, brother helping brother, serving our own kind, "there's no old girls left."

The room is noisy; they used to pipe in music from the radio, except people would come by and change the station to rap. All the while, children would scream, running around the tables playing chase with their older brothers and sisters. The din became impossible to speak over, so they pulled the speakers out. A small Latino boy catches his baby brother who is near Marcus's chair and the little boy lets out a wail that makes Marcus scrunch his face from the child's piercing cry. Behind me, at another table, I can hear an African American straight male complaining that he wants to move from his Section 8 apartment to another low-rent housing project on the Westside, but he needs some sort of documentation to maintain his rental subsidies and if he doesn't get the paperwork he needs he's gonna make that "lazy ass" caseworker of his damn sorry for it. Marcus doesn't have low rent or Section 8. I was lucky to have a friend who got me a cheap apartment.

At the check-in desk, a man is yelling above the whole room. He's cursing that he's had to fucking come all the way back down here because the food bank worker forgot to put into his bag the lunch meat he checked off on the paperwork. Now he's had to waste his time traveling to and from his home and the least they could do would be give him some extra meat and the snack choice again, for compensation. The man is near spitting in the young Latina's face. Marcus leans over and says, "What does he expect, it's free to begin with." He then tells me the guy's a drug addict, used to come into his AA meeting and plunder the refreshments while the meeting was going. Afterwards, he'd bring up his court-issued attendance card to be signed by the secretary, not once having sat down, pulling all kinds of shit on the older queens, getting them to lend him money or take him across town. The Latina at the desk apologizes and apologizes.

My own mind seems to wander after a little while. I stare at the others, the transsexual with a bad wig and torn stockings, the large group of immigrants huddled around the same tables, seemingly embarrassed, their wives commanding a small brood of under-five-year-olds. The few gay men that are there seem so far removed from myself. "Riffraff," Marcus calls them. They wear shoddy clothing from the '80s and acid-washed jeans, concert T-shirts of Aerosmith and Van Halen. Their hair is bed rustled. The skinniest blond is wearing leopard skin Van tennis shoes with holes near the toes. I look at my own hands, notice a bit of dirt lodged under a nail and clean it out quickly. I brush imaginary dirt off the front of my shirt. I don't feel a part of these people either, their emaciated limbs, chronic hacking coughs, their manners rude and demanding. I tell myself I can't believe I've fallen so low that I'm in the same boat as these people. But as I sigh, thinking of how bare my refrigerator is, I know I need the handout as much as they do.

After I put my groceries away, I notice Marcus is distant, gathering the unwashed shirts and socks he's left in my apartment after he's spent the night. At first, I think nothing of it as I start making tuna fish sandwiches for us, squeezing the oil out of the tin, the kitchen smelling of tuna. He looks at what I'm doing and asks for the porn tapes he's left, *Power Tool II* and *Black and Ready*.

I wipe my hands on a kitchen cloth, go into the living room on my hands and knees under the TV. I tell him, "You don't need to watch them if you spend the night here." Marcus says nothing, as angry as he was this morning. Hooking my finger underneath his button fly, I ask, "What's wrong?"

He answers sharply, "Nothing," and pulls my hand away from his crotch. "All I'm good for is sex. I have things to do, my own life." At first, I get angry back, go into the kitchen to finish the sandwiches and again I can hear him looking around. This time he yells out, "Where's my chain with the crystals?"

Again, I go to where I placed it, on the corner of the bedroom mirror. I ask, "Is that all?"

VII

A part of us will survive after we're gone.

BIRTH

"I conjure you, Armisael, angel who governs the womb, that you help this woman and the child in her body."
— JOSHUA TRACHTENBERG, *Jewish Magic and Superstition*

I FEEL IT well up inside of me. It grows with every pass of the sun, steals what little energy is left in my beleaguered body. The lesions that spread daily across my testicles and legs now cease to multiply. I sense the formation of an umbilical cord connecting me to another. I am nervous of what it will become and how it will decimate the remnants of my strength. I tell my lover I am carrying a child inside me; demon-like it drags embryonic nails slowly down my internal organs.

Marcus looks skeptical, eyes squint as if thinking what next, commit me to a home, send me to a spiritual healer? He smolders sage and copal, washes me in their cleansing smoke. He strikes bells to startle me out of my stupefaction but realizes the presence inside me, glides his hand across my stomach, enjoys electricity. In a fit of anger he yells, "How selfish can you be? What if you die before the child is raised?" The neighbors bring sprigs of baby's breath, castor bean stems, and nail them to our door. The air smells rancid and cloying.

I will name the creature Armisael. The growing fetus confines me on my balcony at all hours reciting Psalms. I burn news articles one at a time on the hibachi: the volcanic eruption on modern Pompeii, a killer virus emerging from the rainforest, the increase of rabid coyotes filtering into the hillside communities, feasting on small children. The strips of newsprint writhe in my hand as they approach the fire, like Swedish fortune fish curling inside a palm's heat. I see an indigo gleam radiating from my fingertips; it garners tear-shaped flames, encapsulating the ardor like the many pills I take. They float away into the atmosphere the way soap bubbles defy gravity, lyrical as Ptolemy's *music of the spheres*.

Walking down the boulevards near my home, I expect the community to revere me, to step aside out of deference. Rather, lips snarl, hands move to strike, filthy looks, the kind I imagine Jesus encountered on his trek to Calvary. The women are the harshest, spitting before me, hacking their phlegm deeply and loudly from inside their corpulent bodies. They turn in disgust as if to deny my existence and my child's potential. It is hard to ignore my aspect, my withered limbs seem to negate any fruitfulness. Still the jacaranda trees blanket the sidewalks with their purple flowers for me; the elms canopy the sun's glare, limbs low enough to grab and even cradle me when I tire.

Returning home, I must lie down. Nausea overwhelms me throughout the day. The only thing that helps is placing ice packs underneath my arms and on the back of my neck. My head swims with sounds: the voice of Minnie Riperton, the beating of Navajo drums, the buzz of EMF high-tension lines. Marcus hangs crystal prisms in the bedroom windows and lights cinnamon candles around our bed. He touches me too gently, nuzzling into my side. He licks the well of my ear, says I taste bitter. He wants to gather me up tighter, his arm a vise around my waist. He is afraid he will hurt me, cause some deformation to the child.

The child becomes apparent through translucent skin, jade eyes seem conscious, pierce the iridescence of the amniotic sac. My lover thinks he is a lowly Joseph, not important in the scheme of this miracle. I watch him stare off into the horizon, the sunset nearly blinding. In his hand a cigarette burns, smoke coils from his fingers. He worries about what kind of parent would he be and sees all his flaws magnified, especially his lack of patience. I desire to comfort him, go down on my knees and press my face next to his crotch. Strongly, he pulls me up, tells me it's a piece of immortality, a part of us will survive after we're gone. I warn him not to become too attached, that there might be a chance the child will catch my disease and die early too. Marcus refuses to hear, says he can already see the changes in the world: the sky becoming gentian, the foliage smaragdine, the land ginger. From where I stand, I see darkness drain the landscape's hue, leave somber details, an industrial fog, thick and noxious.

In my dream, I place the child in a basket and float it down a mighty river. Marcus rages at heaven for what I have done, curses me till the day of his death. The child shall never know his real fathers or have comfort with the toys we would have made, our faces appearing god-like over his crib. How can an infected man like me be worthy of this blessing?

I do not know if the little one will appear launched from my head or emerge from the muscles of my legs. But when the moment happens it will be as if a part of me dies. When I release him to the river I will surely crumble to the ground, crying out for Marcus, my body disintegrating into the stuff of protons, neutrons, quarks, shattering back into the dark matter of an unforgiving universe.

LAST SUPPER

Phillip and Matthew's tongues are locked.
They spread themselves over plates and knives,
the dinner table shakes,
and the wine spills over.
I am the one tearing the bread
While my sweet Judas is across
peeling back the petals
till he reaches the heart.
There is butter in his smile.

Later among the olive trees,
the river's bend, the shepherd's crook,
we meet secretly.
I can still taste his soft wool,
legs wrapped in linen
and the hill bedded with ripe fruit
that oiled the skin.
Alone, we thought that nothing could break
our world of bushes and night,
the body safe in nature.
Our shadows grew bold
as the Pharisee approached
with lanterns and clubs.
They carried the temple's footstones
tested the rock's weight, solid in hand

like a ball game, or how children
corner a small animal, ready to pelt.

THE MIRACULOUS CATCH OF FISH

Someone has told Peter that I am on the shore,
faded into the bluff and shells.
He stands unfurled in a small boat,
a sail breathing bare,
a body polished by sun and sweat.
He grabs for a shirt,
arms hide in the sleeves,
his fists come out to fight.

Even now I imagine his hands upon me,
his fingers on my delicate parts,
tracing the wound below the heart and cage,
the clavicle and ilium scratched in salt.
On the sand, he stares through my eyes
avoids the purple marks, stains from my crown,
leaves to build a moss fire.
He tells me to eat, that he loves me
and I cannot stomach either.
My mouth has withered, my lips are dried.
I have no appetite for fish.

FLIGHT

A MAN HAS tied his lover to their bed. The fine silk ropes, with French tassels, have gold filaments woven among the black threads. They catch the light coming from under cloud cover and don't cut into the lover's wrists. The ropes, once used to tie open the heavy velvet curtains in the front room, now are more useful here. They keep the lover from tipping over the soup, chicken noodle, resting on his chest. A wet circle slowly appears where the bowl rests on the napkin.

The lover has short, dark, wavy hair pasted to his scalp. Sweat beads along the sides of the lover's neck and down his bare chest, to his pubic hair just below the navel. He looks as if fever has threaded its way through vein and artery. Ice packs are underneath his armpits. The man blows on the spoon; steam fogs his glasses, his sight becoming dream-like. The lover can only move his arms and legs a mere inch in any direction. Breath, his body's only motion. With each spoonful, the man coos to the lover as one would to an unruly child. The man blows again on the spoon. A tinge of frustration rolls over the man's tongue; he imagines the taste of blood in his mouth.

The lover has been trying to open his mouth to say something, some insignificant word; he will not be persuaded to hush. More likely another demented phrase. Instead, the man shoves the spoon in quickly before the lover has a chance. Broth seeps out the corner of the lover's mouth. Noodles hang over teeth. "This is going nowhere!" the man finally admits and flings the sunny yellow Fiestaware bowl out the window, finally committing to try to understand the utterances of his lover.

The man looks back at where he's thrown the bowl, thinks it's a trick of the mind, the bowl only appearing to float on a current of air. The day's light drizzle ceases for the moment. The man turns to his lover. Yells, "What is so important that it can't wait; why can't you just eat?"

The lover's mouth is cracked and dry; a new package of lemon swab sticks is on the dresser table. Paper cups are stacked and sealed in cellophane. The man moves closer. He can remember how his lover's lips used to feel; now they are ugly scabs and sores. The man also remembers how easy it was to read his lover; he would understand exactly what the lover was thinking through the simplest of gestures.

Now it is more difficult. The man has to beg the lover to repeat, his eyebrow cocked as if the lover was crazy. The man hears the word "love" and is too afraid of its meaning now. He asks the lover to speak again. The lover doesn't repeat; his body arches as if some mystical part has made its escape through the belly.

The man leans out the window to scream for help, but the sky has darkened. Hundreds of bowls are floating out of windows, up and down their street and across town. The man sees the rain being caught by the upright bowls. Signs seem to flash inside his body, telling him that the end has come, his posture changing, sharp and erect, nothing holding him down, his shoulders light as wings. Stranger still, the sensation that the man knows he can fly, as an angel would, to any part of the world, Ecuador, Thailand, the Ivory Coast, and live all over again, without the bind of fear or the weight of responsibility. He closes his lover's eyes, places heavy coins upon the lids, and leaves by the window. The curtains billow.

WAITING

The chairs are comfortable
in this waiting room, gray fabric,
royal blue flecks, meditative lithographs
on the wall. I read poems
out of old *New Yorkers*, legs crossed
tightly, each fragment of poetry
becomes more confused, pastoral.

It has been a month since I last saw the doctor
and always some new thing to watch for,
a thyroid problem prods me to sleep
all afternoon, magnesium and potassium counts low
but nothing I can die from.
I wish I could light a cigarette, watch smoke
curl in the atmosphere. Instead, more patients
flutter in like birds, crash into chairs.
We stare at each other, wonder what we're here for
and how much longer will we have to wait.

The doorknob to the doctor's office turns slowly to click
and the nurse whispers my name in a discreet manner.
I want to question her why she spoke so softly,
should I be ashamed I'm ill, my name a visible lesion.
The poem in the waiting room comes back to me, the pear
hanging off the tree, the color ripe,

skin pocked, brown spots, ready to fall
The doctor helps me onto the scale
firm hand on my elbow and still
more weight slides down, numbers drop.
He tells me my heart is racing and I make excuses—
gym, finishing errands all day—my chest thumps visibly.
He thunders his diagnosis, "Get an echocardiogram!"
A new thing to worry about, another pill,
my growing medicine cabinet crashes full into the sink.

At the end of my visit, I tell him I'm fine,
no, really, I am fine, and if I could borrow
this rolled-up *New Yorker* I'll return it next time.
It'll be a while before I can read the poem thoroughly,
comprehend what each line means, in a way
it assures I'm coming back, that I have at least
another month.

PENANCE

I KNEEL BEFORE the warm wooden altar, can taste the heat from bodies in remorse. This is my favorite crucifixion; the cloth around Jesus' waist hangs just above the beginning curves of the penis, the features are Semitic, arms stretched out in anguish. I have seen many altars. I have knowledge of the things that go into making a crucifix, the angle of the neck, the color of blood, will the eyes follow? More importantly, is the feeling miraculous or tragic or simply kitsch?

Around the edges of the pews, dust collects. I can see an open missal; it asks for prayers to be sent for the ill. The fathers in long robes walk nervously around, up and down aisles, across pews. Lint gathers on the hems; their feet shuffle like they have no purpose. I can see their old, wrinkled hands clutching at each other; sweat starts above their lips. I smell camphor.

The oldest comes up behind me, whispers something into the back of my head, then moves away. At first, I want to strike at him as I would a fly, but I know what he wants, even though I can't understand a thing he has said. All the fathers' eyes stay on me. Inside the church, someone has dimmed the lights; another begins to lock the doors. I follow the elder father. The room is bare except for a large wooden cross propped up by rope and pulley, angled like Caravaggio's *Entombment of Christ*. Large metal spikes have been nailed to the corners. The father removes his clothes carefully, folding them as if freshly washed. I can see scars up and down his back, whipping marks, red and old. His body is devoid of hair and in some ways looks like a child's. His skin smells of burnt pine and kerosene. The soles of his feet are blackened.

He stretches his body onto the cross, his hands and feet grasping the nails. He looks over at me and says he's ready.

I respond, "Bless me father for I have sinned. It has been years since my last confession." The father writhes as if in pleasure. I hide the small gesture of a smile, tell him the most outrageous lies. "I let a woman lick my ass after I shitted. I placed my penis into the mouth of a child and choked him. I pretended a man's penis was the host, said the body and blood of Christ, let the man's cum into open sores in my mouth."

Now the father is really going at it; he shakes his head, nearly loses his grip on the nails. "Please, stop, don't, no more, I can't take it." I tell him more, going slowly, thoroughly describing the scent, the taste, the feel of each transgression. I let him know of the regrets I have afterward, releasing the grip around my lover's neck too soon, how I don't bite nearly as hard as I should. His body arches, consumed as if on fire. I implore the name of Jesus. Finally, tears come rolling down his face, chest heaving, penis erect.

"You are forgiven," he yells. I imagine what it would be like to be fucked by him, his shaft curved upwards like a pig's. These little thoughts keep me from going crazy. The father climbs off the cross and reaches into his trouser pockets, "A little something extra," drops four silver coins into my open hand.

As he leaves, I can see that a line has formed, fathers and sisters, trying to peek into the room. I turn away from them. Next is a man, dark like myself, Puerto Rican or Cuban. This will be a little harder, I surmise, his walk, self-assured, the stature of a connoisseur. I watch as this new father begins to disrobe.

Now is when I work. His fingers tweak the beads of his rosary; my stack of coins begins to rise.

THE CUTTING GARDEN

He is like an old lady: wooden clogs,
white garden gloves, wide-brimmed hat,
halo of spun straw gold.

I am on the old swing bench,
chipped white paint inside my palm.
Just like all the other Westport homes.
My Beloved cuts the peonies,
Teacup roses and bearded irises,

She nags me to paint the porch
as if I were still a young man.

(Our lunch is light: brioche,
slices of mild salami.)
The tables overflow with flowers
after he dips the stems
in boiled cool water.

The moss around the garden becomes lush,
a soft blanket, an invitation to sleep forever.

Weeks later, the stems are wilted.
Small petals drop like blood

around the vase, as if to be read—
Tarot or tea leaves. Tragedy divined,
mala suerte, the body, victim to disease.
Dreams never meant to be fulfilled.

WEDDING BANDS AND BONE

No one tends his plants anymore.
Leaves become old men's skin,
stems nothing more than desert brush.
My beloved stares onto his once-personal Eden,
lush with plants he would bring from work.
Now morphine pellets melt under his tongue,
and all I want is for him to have a little warm broth.
I cannot decipher the hieroglyphs of his eyes
or the gasp of his voice as he tries to speak.
He has chosen to die, defeated doctors' promises—
the pills will make him comfortable—
no longer begs for more air, his last breath peaceful.
The watch and calendar are now the enemy,
the virus, the godsend savior.
I check on him every few hours, pour his tablets into my palm
and feel like a murderer. At times I sleep on the couch
pushed into the corner away from the rented hospital bed.
It is always worse when I wake,
wilted leaves for skin, brittle stems for bones.
His hand has slipped through the rail
and on the carpet shines his/our wedding band.
I try to return his brilliant symbol of us, our triumph.
Every finger kissed will not accept the precious metal;
he is nothing more than an unwrapped mummy.
I steal his ring to place on my other hand

as if he will rise again to claim what is his
and I will gladly hand him our sacred vows.
It is then that the chronometer breaks, twig man's
limbs fragment, dead leaves weave around him like bandages.
A sudden breeze comes through the windows
Sweeps my attention away, pulls him like leaves in a whirlwind
till they are gone and all that's left is stillness.

THINGS LEFT

MY BELOVED'S DRESSER is solid oak and sturdy as a planted tree. The wood has distinctive grain patterns like an alluvial stream. The drawers roll out with the ease of sweet butter or pistons in a new car.

My dresser, however, is not meant to be seen; it is like the ugly daughter in a house of glamorous women having to walk down a spiral staircase to meet a guest. Before Marcus and I moved in together, my dresser was safely tucked away in the closet, and only I knew of its secret life, like Anne Frank hiding from the Nazis of style, crouching silently in the dark. The closet of our new apartment, with all its racks and bars reaching well above my height, cannot fit this dresser, no matter how I try to twist it in. I'm sure the designer of this closet was stricken with a compulsive disorder; he could not stop twitching in delight with each new rod or shelf. So now this poor, plain, white-laminated, particleboard dresser blushes at its unseemly exposure, like a victim on *Cops*, wishing for a fuzzy grid pattern to hide her face.

Having waited three months to see if a miracle would occur—a sudden thunderstorm and Marcus's life would be restored as Lazarus walking back to me in rain-soaked clothes, smelling of heaven—I came to the conclusion that my dresser was hideous in the bedroom. Martha Stewart would have a hard time figuring a way to make it decent and, in head-hung resignation, surrender and just say, Throw it away. A chaise longue, like the one in *Mommy Dearest* during the scene where Joan Crawford slips on a pair of nylons quite seductively, would be a far better functional item. Besides, I have my eye on a tiger-patterned lounge chair I really need. Anyway, Marcus' dresser is much more pleasing. Yes, I am a cad, abandoning the ugly girl who has given me such decent service all this time. I'm sure, in her own way, her eyes are filled with tears, tears running down the sides of her face.

Marcus's dresser is arranged differently than mine. I can't figure out his system, similar to my computer with all these programs that scratch the butts of any computer buff. His top drawer consists of white T-shirts; second drawer, underwear; third drawer, colored T-shirts; fourth, stationery, watercolors, markers, envelopes, and a wax sealer. Bottom drawer is socks.

My dresser is completely different: socks on top, with cards and notes Marcus sent to me even though we lived together. Second drawer consists of underwear; third and fourth, T-shirts, mixed colors and white; bottom, short pants. This is the order I put things on after I take my shower: T-shirt is now on top; it's the first item I put on, since I get cold with my chest bare; underwear next and then finally socks. Voilá! So, if I put it in Marcus's order, I have to put my socks on first, or I could flip the whole pile, but somehow it feels perverted and makes my stomach curdle like when I have to clean the kitten's litter box. It's something I just don't like.

I start with my clothes first, giving that possibility of a miracle just a bit more time. It is a simple project: get rid of anything with holes, or that's too faded or totally pathetic. Like discarded candy wrappers strewn in public waste cans, I have a tall kitchen bag filled with ratty clothes of all kinds. I wonder if my supposed good taste was a fantasy spurred on by a subscription to *GQ*.

Next is the harder part. I had been in Marcus's drawers before, wearing his shirts to bed, drawing with his colored pens. I even feel through his underwear drawer, the rub of the cotton against my hands and fingers makes me shiver like when a fingernail unexpectedly runs down your back. Memories roll in like a fog of us, warm summer nights and crisp cool sheets, the taste of his body, the roughness of his hands embarrassing me.

Now I have a much different purpose, to get rid of unwanted clothes and condense our two dressers into one. As I go through the white T-shirts, I notice yellowed fabric, different style cuts, some still very white, others like old camellias wilting on the branch. As I look down at my hands, I notice I clench every article as if fighting with an identical twin brother, stretching things out of shape in order not to let go, but the dark green plastic bag just bulges with growth like an overzealous gardener and his compost pile. Next, his briefs; this is much easier: blowouts, yellow crotch stains, ripped hems, frayed weave. I can't imagine what he must have done to cause so much damage. Did he scooch around on the living room floor in just his underwear when I wasn't there? Did he sit on the toilet and pee through his jockeys? Did he twist the fabric sitting on the bed until the white seams tore? The possibilities seem endless; out they went. Fortunately, he had recently bought quite a few colored Calvin Klein briefs.

The first time we slept together and undressed, he was shocked that I wasn't wearing tiger-striped bikini underwear or some other funky-patterned thong. It seemed Marcus had a penchant for Latinos, and the common thread they all shared was they wore those tube bikini underwear, the kind you find at K-Mart, Target, or the garment district. I was shocked that a grown man with strands of gray hair running through his hair and mustache still wore boyish little white briefs. Actually, that turned me on; I called him my little boy who I wanted to corrupt, even though he was eight years older. But seeing him like that made him look deceptively innocent, a Little Nikita, or a child actor capable of firing the entire crew.

Marcus had an eye for color; he always seemed to find the most striking T-shirts, like an array of pansies, beautiful oranges, non-obscene purples, greens that did not look military. I only got rid of one shirt that had a spaghetti sauce stain that I remember him getting after I served it to him for dinner. With a ladle in my hand dripping from the bottom, I poured the sauce on the pasta and then plop. Only later did I discover he hated spaghetti. Bad memory.

As I sort through the socks, again I am struck by the awesome palette of colors, from big puffy boot socks to smaller dress socks. A few I couldn't remember him ever wearing—the argyles, the black nylon business pairs, strangers in my apartment. Many of the soles were brownish. He'd wear these socks to work at the nursery, standing in a wet puddle of soil, high enough to soak through his shoes. He made the most beautiful moss baskets and wreaths. Wistfully, I can see again the kind of Zen aura that surrounded him while he worked, not realizing that I had arrived for lunch. As I put my stuff with his, close the drawers, sit on the edge of my bed in my bedroom, I feel he really would have appreciated me getting rid of that ugly white dresser, but with foot-tapping impatience, he would have wanted me to have done this earlier.

1-800-BELOVED

Ring, Ring, Ring
I've already spoken to Marlena and Audrey
but today, Tallulah:
"Hello, Darling, how may I direct your call, Darling?"
I am put on hold, my Marcus paged.
They play recorded music, "Joy to the World,"
done with sitars and African drum.
There is a choir of songbirds, their colors embrace me
like a Mayan royal cape.

My forehead ignites, white light
streams across the crown of my head.
I am intoxicated with the scents of lavender and pumpkin spice.
And then his voice is on the line,
clear and strong, no longer garbled,
drenched with the virus's muddy stormwater.
My mouth tastes the cold sweat of loneliness
and I hesitate,
"Baby, is that you?"

But I am the baby, crying for something indescribable.
He cannot answer my questions;
he can only say he loves me, be strong.
The line clicks far too early, my ears buzz
with the worst memories of his passing.

The phone line doesn't accept credit cards;
the only debt is the crying, the screaming,
the tears that scar the face, the nausea, the refusal to live,
and the strength of my legs still walking this bitter earth.

Afterword

PABLO ALVAREZ

SKIES ARE CHOKED with black helicopters. A statue of Mary is missing its hands. The squawk of parrots renders a whole neighborhood sleepless. A boy ignites a fire with his father's cologne. This collection, *My Body Is Paper*, stands as a poignant tribute to Gil Cuadros's literary prowess and his unyielding spirit in the face of adversity. In poems and stories, retrieved from his archive after his untimely death from AIDS, Cuadros's unique voice and unapologetic narratives provide an intimate window to his sacred sexuality, his queerness, and AIDS.

Cuadros's invocation of sexuality, resistance, and creation will resonate with readers of his first collection, *City of God*. In the story "Hands," which opens *My Body Is Paper*, Cuadros honors the possibility of a loving mother, unlike the narrator's own, making peace with familial damage in the way the narrator admires Yolanda's commitment to her son. "On Yoli's face, I saw a pride I wished my own parents could give me." Cuadros presents a loyal mother, one who comes to understand her son's suffering and does not reject it; rather, she honors it by continuing the ritual work of tending the earth that her son once did, ceremoniously, before his suicide.

Hands become a metaphor for ritual. Across the street from the nursery where his lover works stands a church. There, the narrator witnesses La Señora pulling weeds from the grounds and planting plastic flowers. So intent is her devotion that he is propelled to join her. With the repetitive motion of cultivating the earth, the narrator's hands begin to ache. "It was very quiet work," Cuadros writes. "I started to notice the meditative quality of working this soil . . . that I became more spirit than being." Energy is exchanged through ritual. Through the meditative quality of earth work, of dirt work, Yolanda reveals the story of her son, Trulio, who once tended these same grounds. In "Hands," Cuadros creates an eco-poetic space that calls upon storytelling and the body's ability to transcend the physical, the logical. Anticipating his own death, Cuadros becomes attentive to that divine existence.

The imagery of hands recurs throughout *My Body Is Paper*. Hands of queer fatherhood, hands of lineage, hands of desire cultivate the spirit in this collection. Departing from a chaotic Mexican Catholic upbringing, Cuadros summons multiple forms of spirituality that facilitate healing for the narrator, for Cuadros, and by extension for the reader. Drawing from Indigenous ancestral practices such as burning copal or taking herbal spiritual baths, Cuadros distinguishes Christianity from the divine, revealing an awareness of Chicano identity through queer spirituality rooted in cosmic possibilities and ritual.

I was sixteen when I first discovered that the local bookstore had a section of gay and lesbian authors. I immediately made it a ritual to look for other Chicanx queer writers and storytellers who could inform my Brown queer heritage. I was searching for a writer who could, with conviction, cut to the core about Chicano queer love, who could tell the truth about familial yearning and rejection, a writer who questioned authority. I was searching for Brown, queer literary legacy, a multidimensional pathway to belonging.

After years of searching, the day came when my index finger stopped at the name Gil Cuadros. I slid the book from its shelf and read the title, *City of God*. On the first page, first paragraph, I read the word "Mexico." I drove home that night captivated by the pages I devoured while waiting at red lights. Cuadros's short stories and poetry reflected a reality that spoke to me: Stories of Brown familial loyalties and betrayals, Brown queer desire and imagination, queer spirituality and queer care and AIDS, grounded in Los Angeles, propelled me to keep reading through the night into the early morning hours. I read

some pages over and over. I read other pages in secret; certain sto-
ries were difficult for me to read because they spoke of my own Brown
queer desires in a time when fear-based messages about AIDS and
queer people were constantly being transmitted through major media
outlets.

Discovering Cuadros's work allowed me to question how identity
had been distorted in my academic readings of Chicano sexuality. The
work I read in college relied on social scientists who embarked upon
understanding Chicano queer sexuality through a Euro-American
lens, insensitive to Latinx languages and cultures. They borrowed
from critical theories that privileged a Euro-American gay movement.
While most Anglo gay men were depicted as having unlimited access
to an American landscape with racialized and class privilege, Latino
and Chicano queer men were portrayed as the exotic "other" vaga-
bonding the American playing field in search of sex. However, in *City
of God*, the objectification and eroticization of the Chicano queer have
been repositioned, and I was guided back to my understanding of the
written word as tool and proof of Brown queer sacred sexuality. I was
affirmed in all the complexities and intersections of Chicano queer
identity.

As a graduate student in Chicana and Chicano Studies, I began to
write about Cuadros. I interviewed Terry Wolverton, who had been
Cuadros's writing teacher, and Kevin Martin, his former partner and
executor of his literary estate. Martin let me know that he had been
storing a three-drawer filing cabinet that contained Cuadros's writ-
ing pre- and post-*City of God*. As we celebrated the 25th anniversary of
that groundbreaking collection, the four of us—Martin, Wolverton,
UCLA professor of English Rafael Pérez-Torres, and myself—made
the decision to explore the Cuadros archive to see whether there was
enough work for a second collection. It is significant that Cuadros did
not stop writing once *City of God* was published in 1994. He wrote rig-
orously until he no longer had the strength. And like many in search of
ancestry, I wanted to keep reading.

My Body Is Paper explores the roots of Cuadros's resistance with his political awareness of location, history, and the spaces he occupies. He writes from the city of Los Angeles, the greater geography in which queer youth explore intimacies on the vacant lot of a steam electrical plant or at a park above the foothills where the city lights in the valley provide safety and care. A geography in which lovers read the future by the way rose petals remain in the bathtub after the draining of water and where transients find God at the laundromat on a Friday night.

Stories emerging from Los Angeles take the reader through the impact of AIDS on the body when experimental drugs and side effects send the narrator into delirium and operating rooms. The care of lovers for the ailing writer is made visible in this collection. It is revealed in the poem "Recovery," as the feet of a lover are wrapped and entangled in the tubes of an IV line. A lover's commitment and care offer a source of transcendence for the narrator's AIDS-related surgery, "Kevin's strength is there for me; / I imagine he could cradle me in his arms. / I am that light." The body in this collection is never in hiding. It is nourished by ancient traditions, by the natural environment, by the care of lovers. And while under attack and surveilled by the state, weakened by illness and recovery, the body is in a state of perpetual transcendence. The city becomes witness.

Queer futurity, to exist beyond the trope of survival, brings the book full circle. "Birth" is one of the last literary works by Cuadros. This story regards a critical time in the AIDS epidemic through the death of a genderqueer poz father and the simultaneous birth of his son, Armisael. Disregarding and challenging the gender binary, Cuadros extends the possibility of pregnancy to the narrator. Cuadros writes about two men, both living with HIV, embarking upon parenthood. Surprised by the creation, the narrator's partner questions the survival of both the child and his lover in the face of AIDS: "How selfish can you be? What if you die before the child is raised?"

Carrying the child inside his belly, the narrator undergoes a break-down of the body throughout the narrative; however, despite his deteriorating health, there is new life growing, thriving, within him. The ability to create during this time of AIDS is crucial. The narrator takes pride in his pregnancy and expects from society nothing less than complete respect and admiration for his creation. Yet, he receives glares of disgust, the reminders of a crude civilization unwilling to accept his existence and embrace the possibility of his child's potential in this world.

As the child continues to grow, the narrator's lover begins to see himself as a parent, and his world becomes an Eden, an eternal myth of their creation, "I watch him stare off into the horizon, the sunset nearly blinding. In his hand a cigarette burns, smoke coils from his fingers. He worries about what kind of parent would he be and sees all his flaws magnified, especially his lack of patience. . . . Strongly, he pulls me up, tells me it's a piece of immortality, a part of us will survive after we're gone."

According to the date at the bottom of a hand-typed manuscript in his archive, "Birth" was continuously revised up until nine months before Cuadros's passing in 1996. While most writing of AIDS at the time dealt with the horrific impact of the crisis on the body and the devastating prognosis of immediate death, Cuadros betrays the dominant narrative; his character gives birth to a child who is placed in a basket and released to a mighty river. This child offers an opportunity to mourn what could have been, while offering the possibility of a new world to come once the child is found.

My Body Is Paper fuels the futurity of Chicanx queer literature, ruptures the one-dimensional literary canon of AIDS in the US, and simultaneously affirms the importance of art, resistance, and community in a nation that continues to attempt to erase the legacies of transgender people, queer people, queer people of color, and AIDS. Some of the themes found throughout the collection, such as state betrayal and surveillance, accessible health care, and environmental racism, are as relevant today as they were when Cuadros was writing thirty years ago. His conviction to write truths about queer love, queer care, and queer spirituality is still very much needed.

The child in "Birth" would be twenty-eight years old at the time of the publication of *My Body Is Paper*. Does he know the legacy of his father? Would he know how much his fathers loved him? What hatred has he witnessed? What love has he endured? Will the larger landscape of AIDS and Chicanx communities recognize this child as legacy beyond survival? This collection serves as testament to the child's literary lineage, a heritage. One hope is that future generations of Chicanx and Latinx and queer people will find their own child, their inner child, in the pages of *My Body Is Paper*. That in their search for ancestry, this collection offers a grounding and a departure to the horizon.

Acknowledgments

THE EDITORS would like to gratefully acknowledge Amy Scholder, editor supreme, and Elaine Katzenberger, Publisher of City Lights, for their enthusiasm and their early and ongoing support for bringing Gil's writing into the world; Stacey Lewis, VP, Director of Publicity, Marketing and Sales at City Lights, for her generosity and ingenuity in raising awareness of this book; Robert Drake, for being Gil's book agent and getting *City of God* into print; and Justin Torres, for writing a memorable and heartfelt essay for this book.

We are deeply appreciative of Christopher Velasco and Sybil Venegas of the Laura Aguilar Trust of 2016, for granting permission to reprint Laura's images of Gil; Lizeth Zepeda, University Archivist, Loyola Marymount University, for initiating, with great care, queer of color archival methods; and Michael C. Oliveira, MLIS, of the One Archives at the USC Libraries, for ensuring access to the Gil Cuadros Collection.

About the Author

GIL CUADROS (1962–1996) was a groundbreaking queer Chicanx writer whose work explored the intersections of sexuality, race, and spirituality. Diagnosed as HIV-positive in 1987, Cuadros channeled his experiences into his acclaimed collection *City of God* (published by City Lights in 1994), which captured the raw emotions of living with a life-threatening illness. His lyrical intensity and unflinching honesty shined a light on marginalized communities and familial expectations. The book was highly acclaimed when it was first published and captured the attention of prominent writers in the literary community, among them Paul Monette, Eloise Klein Healy, and Wanda Coleman. In the thirty years since, *City of God* has gone on to become a classic of Chicanx literature.

My Body Is Paper is the body of work by Cuadros that was discovered by professors Pablo Alvarez and Rafael Pérez-Torres in the Gil Cuadros Collection at the One Archives at the USC Libraries many years after Cuadros died from AIDS-related illness. This collection represents his writings at the end of his life, which have not been published until now.

During his lifetime, Gil Cuadros published stories and poems in *Indivisible*, *High Risk 2*, and *Blood Whispers*. His work is also on the compact disc *The Verdict and the Violence*. He was awarded the 1991 Brody Literature Fellowship and was one of the first recipients of the PEN Center USA/West grant to writers with HIV. Cuadros was a resident of West Hollywood when he died in 1996 at the age of thirty-four.